THE PHANTOM 'RICKSHAW

THE
PHANTOM 'RICKSHAW
AND OTHER STORIES

By

RUDYARD KIPLING

STANDARD BOOK COMPANY
LONDON   NEW YORK

"PUNJAB EDITION"
ORSAMUS TURNER HARRIS
MCMXXX

PRINTED IN THE
UNITED STATES OF AMERICA

CONTENTS

	PAGE
THE PHANTOM 'RICKSHAW	7
THE STRANGE RIDE OF MORROWBIE JUKES . . .	45
THE RECRUDESCENCE OF IMRAY	83
MY OWN TRUE GHOST STORY	103
AT THE END OF THE PASSAGE	119
THE MAN WHO WOULD BE KING	153
THE MUTINY OF THE MAVERICKS	211

THE PHANTOM 'RICKSHAW

PREFACE

THIS is not exactly a book of downright ghost-stories as the cover makes believe. It is rather a collection of facts that never quite explained themselves. All that the collector is certain of is, that one man insisted upon dying because he believed himself to be haunted; another man either made up a wonderful lie and stuck to it, or visited a very strange place; while the third man was indubitably crucified by some person or persons unknown, and gave an extraordinary account of himself.

The peculiarity of ghost-stories is that they are never told first-hand. I have managed, with infinite trouble, to secure one exception to this rule. It is not a very good specimen, but you can credit it from beginning to end. The other three stories you must take or trust; as I did.

RUDYARD KIPLING.

THE PHANTOM 'RICKSHAW
AND OTHER STORIES

THE PHANTOM 'RICKSHAW

May no ill dreams disturb my rest,
Nor Powers of Darkness me molest.
Evening Hymn.

ONE of the few advantages that India has over England is a great Knowability. After five years' service a man is directly or indirectly acquainted with the two or three hundred Civilians in his Province, all the Messes of ten or twelve Regiments and Batteries, and some fifteen hundred other people of the non-official caste. In ten years his knowledge should be doubled, and at the end of twenty he knows, or knows something about, every Englishman in the Empire, and may travel anywhere and everywhere without paying hotel-bills.

Globe-trotters who expect entertainment as a right have, even within my memory, blunted this open-heartedness, but none the less to-day, if you belong to the Inner Circle and are neither a Bear nor a Black Sheep, all houses are open to you, and our small world is very, very kind and helpful.

Rickett of Kamartha stayed with Polder of Kumaon some fifteen years ago. He meant to stay two nights, but was knocked down by rheumatic fever, and for six weeks disorganized Polder's establishment, stopped Polder's work, and

7

nearly died in Polder's bedroom. Polder behaves as though he had been placed under eternal obligation by Rickett, and yearly sends the little Ricketts a box of presents and toys. It is the same everywhere. The men who do not take the trouble to conceal from you their opinion that you are an incompetent ass, and the women who blacken your character and misunderstand your wife's amusements, will work themselves to the bone in your behalf if you fall sick or into serious trouble.

Heatherlegh, the Doctor, kept, in addition to his regular practice, a hospital on his private account—an arrangement of loose boxes for Incurables, his friend called it—but it was really a sort of fitting-up shed for craft that had been damaged by stress of weather. The weather in India is often sultry, and since the tale of bricks is always a fixed quantity, and the only liberty allowed is permission to work overtime and get no thanks, men occasionally break down and become as mixed as the metaphors in this sentence.

Heatherlegh is the dearest doctor that ever was, and his invariable prescription to all his patients is, "lie low, go slow, and keep cool." He says that more men are killed by overwork than the importance of this world justifies. He maintains that overwork slew Pansay, who died under his hands about three years ago. He has, of course, the right to speak authoritatively, and he laughs at my theory that there was a crack in

Pansay's head and a little bit of the Dark World came through and pressed him to death. "Pansay went off the handle," says Heatherlegh, "after the stimulus of long leave at Home. He may or he may not have behaved like a blackguard to Mrs. Keith-Wessington. My notion is that the work of the Katabundi Settlement ran him off his legs, and that he took to brooding and making much of an ordinary P. & O. flirtation. He certainly was engaged to Miss Mannering, and she certainly broke off the engagement. Then he took a feverish chill and all that nonsense about ghosts developed. Overwork started his illness, kept it alight, and killed him, poor devil. Write him off to the System—one man to take the work of two and a half men."

I do not believe this. I used to sit up with Pansay sometimes when Heatherlegh was called out to patients, and I happened to be within claim. The man would make me most unhappy by describing in a low, even voice, the procession that was always passing at the bottom of his bed. He had a sick man's command of language. When he recovered I suggested that he should write out the whole affair from beginning to end, knowing that ink might assist him to ease his mind. When little boys have learned a new bad word they are never happy till they have chalked it up on a door. And this also is Literature.

He was in a high fever while he was writing, and the blood-and-thunder Magazine diction he

adopted did not calm him. Two months afterwards he was reported fit for duty, but, in spite
of the fact that he was urgently needed to help
an undermanned Commission stagger through a
deficit, he preferred to die; vowing at the last
that he was hag-ridden. I got his manuscript before he died, and this is his version of the affair,
dated 1885:—

My doctor tells me that I need rest and change
of air. It is not improbable that I shall get both
ere long—rest that neither the red-coated mes-
senger nor the midday gun can break, and change
of air far beyond that which any homeward-bound
steamer can give me. In the meantime I am re-
solved to stay where I am; and, in flat defiance of
my doctor's orders, to take all the world into my
confidence. You shall learn for yourselves the
precise nature of my malady; and shall, too, judge
for yourselves whether any man born of woman
on this weary earth was ever so tormented as I.

Speaking now as a condemned criminal might
speak ere the drop-bolts are drawn, my story, wild
and hideously improbable as it may appear, demands at least attention. That it will ever receive
credence I utterly disbelieve. Two months ago
I should have scouted as mad or drunk the man
who had dared tell me the like. Two months ago
I was the happiest man in India. To-day, from
Peshawar to the sea, there is no one more

wretched. My doctor and I are the only two who know this. His explanation is, that my brain, digestion, and eyesight are all slightly affected; giving rise to my frequent and persistent "delusions." Delusions, indeed! I call him a fool; but he attends me still with the same unwearied smile, the same bland professional manner, the same neatly-trimmed red whiskers, till I begin to suspect that I am an ungrateful, evil-tempered invalid. But you shall judge for yourselves.

Three years ago it was my fortune—my great misfortune—to sail from Gravesend to Bombay, on return from long leave, with one Agnes Keith-Wessington, wife of an officer on the Bombay side. It does not in the least concern you to know what manner of woman she was. Be content with the knowledge that, ere the voyage had ended, both she and I were desperately and unreasoningly in love with one another. Heaven knows that I can make the admission now without one particle of vanity. In matters of this sort there is always one who gives and another who accepts. From the first day of our ill-omened attachment, I was conscious that Agnes's passion was a stronger, a more dominant, and—if I may use the expression—a purer sentiment than mine. Whether she recognized the fact then, I do not know. Afterwards it was bitterly plain to both of us.

Arrived at Bombay in the spring of the year, we went our respective ways, to meet no more for the next three or four months, when my leave and her love took us both to Simla. There we spent the season together; and there my fire of straw burnt itself out to a pitiful end with the closing year. I attempt no excuse. I make no apology. Mrs. Wessington had given up much for my sake, and was prepared to give up all. From my own lips, in August, 1882, she learnt that I was sick of her presence, tired of her company, and weary of the sound of her voice. Ninety-nine women out of a hundred would have wearied of me as I wearied of them; seventy-five of that number would have promptly avenged themselves by active and obtrusive flirtation with other men. Mrs. Wessington was the hundredth. On her neither my openly expressed aversion nor the cutting brutalities with which I garnished our interviews had the least effect.

"Jack, darling!" was her one eternal cuckoo cry: "I'm sure it's all a mistake—a hideous mistake; and we'll be good friends again some day. Please forgive me, Jack, dear."

I was the offender, and I knew it. That knowledge transformed my pity into passive endurance, and, eventually, into blind hate—the same instinct, I suppose, which prompts a man to savagely stamp on the spider he has but half killed. And with this hate in my bosom the season of 1882 came to an end.

Next year we met again at Simla—she with her monotonous face and timid attempts at reconciliation, and I with loathing of her in every fiber of my frame. Several times I could not avoid meeting her alone; and on each occasion her words were identically the same. Still the unreasoning wail that it was all a "mistake"; and still the hope of eventually "making friends." I might have seen, had I cared to look, that that hope only was keeping her alive. She grew more wan and thin month by month. You will agree with me, at least, that such conduct would have driven any one to despair. It was uncalled for; childish; unwomanly. I maintain that she was much to blame. And again, sometimes, in the black, fever-stricken night watches, I have begun to think that I might have been a little kinder to her. But that really is a "delusion." I could not have continued pretending to love her when I didn't; could I? It would have been unfair to us both.

Last year we met again—on the same terms as before. The same weary appeals, and the same curt answers from my lips. At least I would make her see how wholly wrong and hopeless were her attempts at resuming the old relationship. As the season wore on, we fell apart—that is to say, she found it difficult to meet me, for I had other and more absorbing interests to attend to. When I think it over quietly in my sick-room, the season of 1884 seems a confused nightmare wherein light and shade were fantastically intermingled—my courtship of little Kitty Mannering; my hopes, doubts, and fears; our long rides together; my trembling avowal of attachment; her reply; and

now and again a vision of a white face flitting by
in the 'rickshaw with the black and white liveries
I once watched for so earnestly; the wave of Mrs.
Wessington's gloved hand; and, when she met me
alone, which was but seldom, the irksome monot-
ony of her appeal. I loved Kitty Mannering;
honestly, heartily loved her, and with my love for
her grew my hatred for Agnes. In August, Kitty
and I were engaged. The next day I met those
accursed "magpie" *jhampanies* at the back of
Jakko, and, moved by some passing sentiment of
pity, stopped to tell Mrs. Wessington everything.
She knew it already.

"So I hear you're engaged, Jack dear." Then,
without a moment's pause:—"I'm sure it's all a
mistake—a hideous mistake. We shall be as good
friends some day, Jack, as we ever were."

My answer might have made even a man wince.
It cut the dying woman before me like the blow
of a whip.

"Please forgive me, Jack; I didn't mean to
make you angry; but it's true, it's true!"

And Mrs. Wessington broke down completely.
I turned away and left her to finish her journey
in peace, feeling, but only for a moment or two,
that I had been an unutterably mean hound. I
looked back, and saw that she had turned her
'rickshaw with the idea, I suppose, of overtaking
me.

The scene and its surroundings were photo-
graphed on my memory. The rain-swept sky (we

were at the end of the wet weather), the sodden, dingy pines, the muddy road, and the black powder-riven cliffs formed a gloomy background against which the black and white liveries of the *jhampanies,* the yellow-paneled 'rickshaw, and Mrs. Wessington's down-bowed golden head stood out clearly. She was holding her handkerchief in her left hand and was leaning back exhausted against the 'rickshaw cushions. I turned my horse up a by-path near the Sanjowlie Reservoir and literally ran away. Once I fancied I heard a faint call of "Jack!" This may have been imagination. I never stopped to verify it. Ten minutes later I came across Kitty on horseback; and, in the delight of a long ride with her, forgot all about the interview.

A week later Mrs. Wessington died, and the inexpressible burden of her existence was removed from my life. I went Plainsward perfectly happy. Before three months were over I had forgotten all about her, except that at times the discovery of some of her old letters reminded me unpleasantly of our bygone relationship. By January I had disinterred what was left of our correspondence from among my scattered belongings and had burnt it. At the beginning of April of this year, 1885, I was at Simla—semi-deserted Simla—once more, and was deep in lover's talks and walks with Kitty. It was decided that we should be married at the end of June. You will understand, therefore, that, loving Kitty as I did, I am not saying too much when I pronounce myself to have been, at that time, the happiest man in India.

Fourteen delightful days passed almost before I noticed their flight. Then, aroused to the sense of what was proper among mortals circumstanced as we were, I pointed out to Kitty that an engagement ring was the outward and visible sign of her dignity as an engaged girl; and that she must forthwith come to Hamilton's to be measured for one. Up to that moment, I give you my word, we had completely forgotten so trivial a matter. To Hamilton's we accordingly went on the 15th of April, 1885. Remember that—whatever my doctor may say to the contrary—I was then in perfect health, enjoying a well-balanced mind and an absolutely tranquil spirit. Kitty and I entered Hamilton's shop together, and there, regardless of the order of affairs, I measured Kitty for the ring in the presence of the amused assistant. The ring was a sapphire with two diamonds. We then rode out down the slope that leads to the Combermere Bridge and Peliti's shop.

While my Waler was cautiously feeling his way over the loose shale, and Kitty was laughing and chattering at my side—while all Simla that is to say as much of it as had then come from the Plains, was grouped round the Reading-room and Peliti's veranda,—I was aware that some one, apparently at a vast distance, was calling me by my Christian name. It struck me that I had heard the voice before, but when and where I could not at once determine. In the short space it took to cover the road between the path from Hamilton's shop and the first plank of the Combermere Bridge I had thought over half a dozen people who might have committed such a solecism, and had eventually decided that it must have been some singing in my ears. Immediately opposite Peliti's shop my eye was arrested by the sight of four *jhampanies* in "magpie" livery, pulling a yellow-paneled, cheap, bazaar 'rickshaw. In a moment my mind flew back to the previous season and Mrs. Wessington with a sense of irritation and disgust. Was it not enough that the woman was dead and done with, without her black and white servitors reappearing to spoil the day's happiness? Whoever employed them now I thought I would call upon, and ask as a personal favor to change her *jhampanies'* livery. I would hire the men myself, and, if necessary, buy their coats from off their backs. It is impossible to say here what a flood of undesirable memories their presence evoked.

"Kitty," I cried, "there are poor Mrs. Wessington's *jhampanies* turned up again! I wonder who has them now?"

Kitty had known Mrs. Wessington slightly last season, and had always been interested in the sickly woman.

"What? Where?" she asked. "I can't see them anywhere."

Even as she spoke, her horse, swerving from

a laden mule, threw himself directly in front of the advancing 'rickshaw. I had scarcely time to utter a word of warning, when, to my unutterable horror, horse and rider passed through men and carriage as if they had been thin air.

"What's the matter?" cried Kitty; "what made you call out so foolishly, Jack? If I am engaged I don't want all creation to know about it. There was lots of space between the mule and the veranda; and, if you think I can't ride—There!"

Whereupon willful Kitty set off, her dainty little head in the air, at a hand-gallop in the direction of the Band-stand; fully expecting, as she herself afterwards told me, that I should follow her. What was the matter? Nothing indeed. Either that I was mad or drunk, or that Simla was haunted with devils. I reined in my impatient cob, and turned round. The 'rickshaw had turned, too, and now stood immediately facing me, near the left railing of the Combermere Bridge.

"Jack! Jack, darling!" There was no mistake about the words this time: they rang through my brain as if they had been shouted in my ear. "It's some hideous mistake, I'm sure. Please forgive me, Jack, and let's be friends again."

The 'rickshaw-hood had fallen back, and inside, as I hope and pray daily for the death I dread by night, sat Mrs. Keith-Wessington, handkerchief in hand, and golden head bowed on her breast.

How long I stared motionless I do not know.

Finally, I was aroused by my syce taking the Waler's bridle and asking whether I was ill. From the horrible to the commonplace is but a step. I tumbled off my horse and dashed, half fainting, into Peliti's for a glass of cherry-brandy. There two or three couples were gathered round the coffee-tables discussing the gossip of the day. Their trivialities were more comforting to me just then than the consolations of religion could have been. I plunged into the midst of the conversation at once; chatted, laughed, and jested with a face (when I caught a glimpse of it in a mirror) as white and drawn as that of a corpse. Three or four men noticed my condition; and, evidently setting it down to the results of over-many pegs, charitably endeavored to draw me apart from the rest of the loungers. But I refused to be led away. I wanted the company of my kind—as a child rushes into the midst of the dinner-party after a fright in the dark. I must have talked for about ten minutes or so, though it seemed an eternity to me, when I heard Kitty's clear voice outside inquiring for me. In another minute she had entered the shop, prepared to roundly upbraid me for failing so signally in my duties. Something in my face stopped her.

"Why, Jack," she cried, "what have you been doing? What has happened? Are you ill?" Thus driven into a direct lie, I said that the sun had been a little too much for me. It was close upon five o'clock of a cloudy April afternoon, and the sun had been hidden all day. I saw my mistake as soon as the words were out of my mouth; attempted to recover it; blundered hopelessly and followed Kitty in a regal rage, out of doors, amid the smiles of my acquaintances. I made some excuse (I have forgotten what) on the score of my feeling faint; and cantered away to my hotel, leaving Kitty to finish the ride by herself.

In my room I sat down and tried calmly to reason out the matter. Here was I, Theobald Jack Pansay, a well-educated Bengal Civilian in the year of grace 1885, presumably sane, certainly healthy, driven in terror from my sweetheart's side by the apparition of a woman who had been dead and buried eight months ago. These were facts that I could not blink. Nothing was further from my thought than any memory of Mrs. Wessington when Kitty and I left Hamilton's shop. Nothing was more utterly commonplace than the stretch of wall opposite Peliti's. It was broad daylight. The road was full of people; and yet here, look you, in defiance of every law of probability, in direct outrage of Nature's ordinance, there had appeared to me a face from the grave.

Kitty's Arab had gone through the 'rickshaw: so that my first hope that some woman marvelously like Mrs. Wessington had hired the carriage and the coolies with their old livery was lost. Again and again I went round this treadmill of thought; and again and again gave up baffled and in despair. The voice was as inexplicable as the apparition. I had originally some wild notion of confiding it all to Kitty; of begging her to marry me at once; and in her arms defying the ghostly occupant of the 'rickshaw. "After all," I argued, "the presence of the 'rickshaw is in itself enough to prove the existence of a spectral illusion. One may see ghosts of men and women, but surely never of coolies and carriages. The whole thing is absurd. Fancy the ghost of a hillman!"

Next morning I sent a penitent note to Kitty, imploring her to overlook my strange conduct of the previous afternoon. My Divinity was still very wroth, and a personal apology was necessary. I explained, with a fluency born of night-long pondering over a falsehood, that I had been attacked with a sudden palpitation of the heart—the result of indigestion. This eminently practical solution had its effect; and Kitty and I rode out that afternoon with the shallow of my first lie dividing us.

Nothing would please her save a canter round Jakko. With my nerves still unstrung from the previous night, I feebly protested against the notion, suggesting Observatory Hill, Jutogh, the Boileaugunge road—anything rather than the Jakko round. Kitty was angry and a little hurt: so I yielded from fear of provoking further misunderstanding, and we set out together towards Chota Simla. We walked a greater part of the way, and according to our custom, cantered from a mile or so below the convent to a stretch of level

road by the Sanjowlie Reservoir. The wretched
horses appeared to fly, and my heart beat quicker
and quicker as we neared the crest of the ascent.
My mind had been full of Mrs. Wessington all the
afternoon; and every inch of the Jakko road bore
witness to our old-time walks and talks. The
bowlders were full of it; the pines sang it aloud
overhead; the rain-fed torrents giggled and
chuckled unseen over the shameful story; and
the wind in my ears chanted the iniquity
aloud.

As a fitting climax, in the middle of the level
men call the Ladies' Mile the Horror was await-
ing me. No other 'rickshaw was in sight—only
the four black and white *jhampanies,* the yellow-
paneled carriage, and the golden head of the
woman within—all apparently just as I had left
them eight months and one fortnight ago! For an
instant I fancied that Kitty must see what I saw
—we were so marvelously sympathetic in all
things. Her next words undeceived me—"Not a
soul in sight! Come along, Jack, and I'll race you
to the Reservoir buildings!" Her wiry little Arab
was off like a bird, my Waler following close behind, and in this order we dashed under the cliffs.
Half a minute brought us within fifty yards of the
'rickshaw. I pulled my Waler and fell back a
little. The 'rickshaw was directly in the middle of
the road; and once more the Arab passed through
it, my horse following. "Jack! Jack dear! Please
forgive me," rang with a wail in my ears, and,

after an interval:—"It's all a mistake, a hideous mistake!"

I spurred my horse like a man possessed. When I turned my head at the Reservoir works, the black and white liveries were still waiting—patiently waiting—under the gray hillside, and the wind brought me a mocking echo of the words I had just heard. Kitty bantered me a good deal on my silence throughout the remainder of the ride. I had been talking up till then wildly and at random. To save my life I could not speak afterwards naturally, and from Sanjowlie to the Church wisely held my tongue.

I was to dine with the Mannerings that night, and had barely time to canter home to dress. On the road to Elysium Hill I overheard two men talking together in the dusk.—"It's a curious thing," said one, "how completely all trace of it disappeared. You know my wife was insanely fond of the woman (never could see anything in her myself), and wanted me to pick up her old 'rickshaw and coolies if they were to be got for love or money. Morbid sort of fancy I call it; but I've got to do what the *Memsahib* tells me. Would you believe that the man she hired it from tells me that all four of the men—they were brothers—died of cholera on the way to Hardwar, poor devils; and the 'rickshaw has been broken up by the man himself. 'Told me he never used a dead *Memsahib's* 'rickshaw. 'Spoilt his luck. Queer notion, wasn't it? Fancy poor little Mrs.

Wessington spoiling any one's luck except her own!" I laughed aloud at this point; and my laugh jarred on me as I uttered it. So there were ghosts of 'rickshaws after all, and ghostly employments in the other world! How much did Mrs. Wessington give her men? What were their hours? Where did they go?

And for visible answer to my last question I saw the infernal Thing blocking my path in the twilight. The dead travel fast, and by short cuts unknown to ordinary coolies. I laughed aloud a second time, and checked my laughter suddenly, for I was afraid I was going mad. Mad to a certain extent I must have been, for I recollect that I reined in my horse at the head of the 'rickshaw, and politely wished Mrs. Wessington "Good evening." Her answer was one I knew only too well. I listened to the end; and replied that I had heard it all before, but should be delighted if she had anything further to say. Some malignant devil stronger than I must have entered into me that evening, for I have a dim recollection of talking the commonplaces of the day for five minutes to the Thing in front of me.

"Mad as a hatter, poor devil—or drunk. Max, try and get him to come home."

Surely that was not Mrs. Wessington's voice! The two men had overheard me speaking to the empty air, and had returned to look after me. They were very kind and considerate, and from their words evidently gathered that I was extremely drunk. I thanked them confusedly and cantered away to my hotel, there changed, and arrived at the Mannering's ten minutes late. I pleaded the darkness of the night as an excuse; was rebuked by Kitty for my unlover-like tardiness; and sat down.

The conversation had already become general; and under cover of it, I was addressing some tender small talk to my sweetheart, when I was aware that at the further end of the table a short red-whiskered man was describing, with much broidery, his encounter with a mad unknown that evening.

A few sentences convinced me that he was repeating the incident of half an hour ago. In the middle of the story he looked around for applause, as professional story-tellers do, caught my eye, and straightway collapsed. There was a moment's awkward silence, and the red-whiskered man muttered something to the effect that he had "forgotten the rest," thereby sacrificing a reputation as a good story-teller which he had built up for six seasons past. I blessed him from the bottom of my heart, and—went on with my fish.

In the fullness of time that dinner came to an end; and with genuine regret I tore myself away from Kitty—as certain as I was of my own existence that It would be waiting for me outside the door. The red-whiskered man, who had been introduced to me as Dr. Heatherlegh of Simla, volunteered to bear me company as far as our

roads lay together. I accepted his offer with
gratitude.

My instinct had not deceived me. It lay in
readiness in the Mall, and, in what seemed devilish mockery of our ways, with a lighted head-lamp.
The red-whiskered man went to the point at once,
in a manner that showed he had been thinking over
it all dinner time.

"I say, Pansay, what the deuce was the matter
with you this evening on the Elysium road?"
The suddenness of the question wrenched an answer from me before I was aware.

"That!" said I, pointing to It.

"That, may be either D. T. or Eyes for aught
I know. Now you don't liquor. I saw as much
at dinner, so it can't be D. T. There's nothing
whatever where you're pointing, though you're
sweating and trembling with fright like a scared
pony. Therefore, I conclude that it's Eyes. And
I ought to understand all about them. Come along
home with me. I'm on the Blessington lower
road."

To my intense delight the 'rickshaw, instead
of waiting for us, kept about twenty yards ahead
—and this, too, whether we walked, trotted, or
cantered. In the course of that long night ride
I had told my companion almost as much as I have
told you here.

"Well, you've spoil one of the best tales I've
ever laid tongue to," said he, "but I'll forgive
you for the sake of what you've gone through.

Now come home and do what I tell you; and when I've cured you, young man, let this be a lesson to you to steer clear of women and indigestible food till the day of your death."

The 'rickshaw kept steady in front; and my red-whiskered friend seemed to derive great pleasure from my account of its exact whereabouts.

"Eyes, Pansay—all Eyes, Brain, and Stomach. And the greatest of these three is Stomach. You've too much conceited Brain, too little Stomach, and thoroughly unhealthy Eyes. Get your Stomach straight and the rest follows. And all that's French for a liver pill. I'll take sole medical charge of you from this hour! for you're too interesting a phenomenon to be passed over."

By this time we were deep in the shadow of the Blessington lower road and the 'rickshaw came to a dead stop under a pine-clad, overhanging shale cliff. Instinctively I halted too, giving my reason, Heatherlegh rapped out an oath.

"Now, if you think I'm going to spend a cold night on the hillside for the sake of a Stomach *cum*-Brain-*cum*-Eye illusion. . . . Lord, ha' mercy! What's that?"

There was a muffled report, a blinding smother of dust just in front of us, a crack, the noise of rent boughs, and about ten yards of the cliff-side —pines, undergrowth, and all—slid down into the road below, completely blocking it up. The uprooted trees swayed and tottered for a moment like drunken giants in the gloom, and then fell prone among their fellows with a thunderous crash.   Our two horses stood motionless and sweating with fear.   As soon as the rattle of falling earth and stone had subsided, my companion muttered:—"Man if we'd gone forward we should have been ten feet deep in our graves by now.   'There are more things in heaven and earth.'   .   .   .   Come home, Pansay, and thank God.   I want a peg badly."

We retraced our way over the Church Ridge, and I arrived at Dr. Heatherlegh's house shortly after midnight.

His attempts towards my cure commenced almost immediately, and for a week I never left his side.   Many a time in the course of that week did I bless the good-fortune which had thrown me in contact with Simla's best and kindest doctor.   Day by day my spirits grew lighter and more equable.   Day by day, too, I became more and more inclined to fall in with Heatherlegh's "spectral illusion" theory, implicating eyes, brain, and stomach.   I wrote to Kitty, telling her that a slight sprain caused by a fall from my horse had kept me indoors for a few days; and that I should be recovered before she had time to regret my absence.

Heatherlegh's treatment was simple to a degree. It consisted of liver pills, cold-water baths, and strong exercise, taken in the dusk or at early dawn—for, as he sagely observed:—"A man with a sprained ankle doesn't walk a dozen miles a day, and your young woman might be wondering if she saw you."

At the end of the week, after much examination of pupil and pulse, and strict injunctions as to diet and pedestrianism, Heatherlegh dismissed me as brusquely as he had taken charge of me. Here is his parting benediction:—"Man, I certify to your mental cure, and that's as much as to say I've cured most of your bodily ailments. Now, get your traps out of this as soon as you can; and be off to make love to Miss Kitty."

I was endeavoring to express my thanks for his kindness. He cut me short.

"Don't think I did this because I like you. I gather that you've behaved like a blackguard all through. But, all the same, you're a phenomenon, and as queer a phenomenon as you are a black-guard. No!"—checking me a second time—"not a rupee, please. Go out and see if you can find the eyes-brain-and-stomach again. I'll give you a lakh for each time you see it."

Half and hour later I was in the Mannerings' drawing-room with Kitty—drunk, with the in-toxication of present happiness and the fore-knowledge that I should never more be troubled with Its hideous presence. Strong in the sense of my new-found security, I proposed a ride at once; and, by preference, a canter round Jakko.

Never had I felt so well, so overladen with vitality and mere animal spirits, as I did on the afternoon of the 30th of April. Kitty was delighted at the change in my appearance, and complimented me on it in her delightfully frank and outspoken manner. We left the Mannerings' house together, laughing and talking, and cantered along the Chota Simla road as of old.

I was in haste to reach the Sanjowlie Reservoir and there make my assurance doubly sure. The horses did their best, but seemed all too slow to my impatient mind. Kitty was astonished at my boisterousness. "Why, Jack!" she cried at last, "you are behaving like a child. What are you doing?"

We were just below the Convent, and from sheer wantonness I was making my Waler plunge and curvet across the road as I tickled it with the loop of my riding-whip.

"Doing?" I answered: "nothing, dear. That's just it. If you'd been doing nothing for a week except lie up, you'd be as riotous as I.

> "'Singing and murmuring in your feastful mirth,
>   Joying to feel yourself alive;
>   Lord over Nature, Lord of the visible Earth,
>   Lord of the senses five.'"

My quotation was hardly out of my lips before we had rounded the corner above the Convent; and a few yards further on could see across to Sonjowlie. In the center of the level road stood the black and white liveries, the yellow-paneled 'rickshaw, and Mrs. Keith-Wessington. I pulled up, looked, rubbed my eyes, and, I believe, must

have said something. The next thing I knew
was that I was lying face downward on the road,
with Kitty kneeling above me in tears.

"Has It gone, child?" I gasped. Kitty only
wept more bitterly.

"Has what gone, Jack dear? What does it all
mean? There must be a mistake somewhere, Jack.
A hideous mistake." Her last words brought me
to my feet—mad—raving for the time being.

"Yes, there is a mistake somewhere," I repeated,
"a hideous mistake. Come and look at It."

I have an indistinct idea that I dragged Kitty
by the wrist along the road up to where It stood,
and implored her for pity's sake to speak to It;
to tell It that we were betrothed; that neither
Death nor Hell could break the tie between us; and
Kitty only knows how much more to the same
effect. Now and again I appealed passionately to
the Terror in the 'rickshaw to bear witness to all
I had said, and to release me from a torture that
was killing me. As I talked I suppose I must
have told Kitty of my old relations with Mrs.
Wessington, for I saw her listen intently with
white face and blazing eyes.

"Thank you, Mr. Pansay," she said, "that's
quite enough. *Syce ghora láo.*"

The syces, impassive as Orientals always are,
had come up with the recaptured horses; and as
Kitty sprang into her saddle I caught hold of the
bridle, entreating her to hear me out and forgive.
My answer was the cut of her riding-whip across

my face from mouth to eye, and a word or two
of farewell that even now I cannot write down.
So I judged, and judged rightly, that Kitty knew
all; and I staggered back to the side of the 'rickshaw. My face was cut and bleeding, and the
blow of the riding-whip had raised a livid blue
weal on it. I had no self-respect. Just then,
Heatherlegh, who must have been following Kitty
and me at a distance, cantered up.

"Doctor," I said, pointing to my face, "here's
Miss Mannering's signature to my order of dis-
missal and . . . I'll thank you for that lakh as
soon as convenient."

Heatherlegh's face, even in my abject misery,
moved me to laughter.

"I'll stake my professional reputation"—he began.

"Don't be a fool," I whispered. "I've lost my
life's happiness and you'd better take me home."

As I spoke the 'rickshaw was gone. Then I
lost all knowledge of what was passing. The crest
of Jakko seemed to heave and roll like the crest
of a cloud and fall in upon me.

Seven days later (on the 7th of May, that is
to say) I was aware that I was lying in Heatherlegh's room as weak as a little child. Heatherlegh
was watching me intently from behind the papers
on his writing-table. His first words were not
encouraging; but I was far too spent to be much
moved by them.

"Here's Miss Kitty has sent back your letters.

You correspond a good deal, you young people. Here's a packet that looks like a ring, and a cheerful sort of a note from Mannering Papa, which I've taken the liberty of reading and burning. The old gentleman's not pleased with you."

"And Kitty?" I asked dully.

"Rather more drawn than her father, from what she says. By the same token you must have been letting out any number of queer reminiscences just before I met you. 'Says that a man who would have behaved to a woman as you did to Mrs. Wessington ought to kill himself out of sheer pity for his kind. She is a hot-headed little virago, your mash. 'Will have it, too, that you were suffering from D. T. when that row on the Jakko road turned up. 'Says she'll die before she ever speaks to you again."

I groaned and turned over on the other side.

"Now you've got your choice, my friend. This engagement has to be broken off; and the Mannerings' don't want to be too hard on you. Was it broken through D. T. or epileptic fits? Sorry I can't offer you a better exchange unless you'd prefer hereditary insanity. Say the word and I'll tell 'em it's fits. All Simla knows about that scene on the Ladies' Mile. Come! I'll give you five minutes to think it over!"

During those five minutes I believe that I explored thoroughly the lowest circles of the Inferno which it is permitted man to tread on earth. And at the same time I myself was watching myself faltering through the dark labyrinths of doubt, misery, and utter despair. I wondered, as Heatherlegh in his chair might have wondered, which dreadful alternative I should adopt. Presently I heard myself answering in a voice that I hardly recognized,—

"They're confoundedly particular about morality in these parts. Give 'em fits, Heatherlegh, and my love. Now let me sleep a bit longer."

Then my two selves joined, and it was only I (half crazed, devil-riven I) that tossed in my bed, tracing step by step the history of the past month.

"But I am in Simla," I kept repeating to myself. "I, Jack Pansay, am in Simla, and there are no ghosts here. It's unreasonable of that woman to pretend there are. Why couldn't Agnes have left me alone? I never did her any harm. It might just as well have been me as Agnes. Only I'd never have come back on purpose to kill her. Why can't I be left alone—left alone and happy?"

It was high noon when I first awoke: and the sun was low in the sky before I slept—slept as the tortured criminal sleeps on his rack, too worn to feel further pain.

Next day I could not leave my bed. Heatherlegh told me in the morning that he had received an answer from Mr. Mannering, and that, thanks to his (Heatherlegh's) friendly offices, the story of my affliction had traveled the length and breadth of Simla, where I was on all sides much pitied.

"And that's rather more than you deserve," he concluded pleasantly, "though the Lord knows you've been going through a pretty severe mill. Never mind; we'll cure you yet, you perverse phenomenon."

I declined firmly to be cured. "You've been much too good to me already, old man," said I; "but I don't think I need trouble you further."

In my heart I knew that nothing Heatherlegh could do would lighten the burden that had been laid upon me.

With that knowledge came also a sense of hopeless, impotent rebellion against the unreasonableness of it all. There were scores of men no better than I whose punishments had at least been reserved for another world; and I felt that it was bitterly, cruelly unfair that I alone should have been singled out for so hideous a fate. This mood would in time give place to another where it seemed that the 'rickshaw and I were the only realities in a world of shadows; that Kitty was a ghost; that Mannering, Heatherlegh, and all the other men and women I knew were all ghosts; and the great, gray hills themselves but vain shadows devised to torture me. From mood to mood I tossed backwards and forwards for seven weary days; my body growing daily stronger and stronger, until the bedroom looking-glass told me that I had returned to every day life, and was as other men once more. Curiously enough my face showed no signs of the struggle I had gone through. It was pale indeed, but as expressionless and common-place as ever. I had expected some permanent alteration—visible evidence of the disease that was eating me away. I found nothing.

On the 15th of May I left Heatherlegh's house at eleven o'clock in the morning; and the instinct of the bachelor drove me to the Club. There I found that every man knew my story as told by Heatherlegh, and was, in clumsy fashion, abnormally kind and attentive. Nevertheless I recognized that for the rest of my natural life I should be among but not of my fellows; and I envied very bitterly indeed the laughing coolies on the Mall below. I lunched at the Club, and at four o'clock wandered aimlessly down the Mall in the vague hope of meeting Kitty. Close to the Bandstand the black and white liveries joined me; and I heard Mrs. Wessington's old appeal at my side. I had been expecting this ever since I came out; and was only surprised at her delay. The phantom 'rickshaw and I went side by side along the Chota Simla road in silence. Close to the bazaar, Kitty and a man on horseback overtook and passed us. For any sign she gave I might have been a dog in the road. She did not even pay me the compliment of quickening her pace; though the rainy afternoon had served for an excuse.

So Kitty and her companion, and I and my ghostly Light-o'-Love, crept round Jakko in cou-

ples.   The road was streaming with water; the
pines dripped like roof-pipes on the rocks below,
and the air was full of fine, driving rain.   Two or
three times I found myself saying to myself almost aloud:—"I'm Jack Pansay on leave at Simla
—at Simla! Every-day, ordinary Simla! I mustn't
forget that—I mustn't forget that."   Then
I would try to recollect some of the gossip I had
heard at the Club; the prices of So-and-So's horses
—anything, in fact, that related to the work-a-day
Anglo-Indian world I knew so well.   I even repeated the multiplication-table rapidly to myself,
to make quite sure that I was not taking leave of
my senses.   It gave me much comfort; and must
have prevented my hearing Mrs. Wessington for
a time.

Once more I wearily climbed the Convent slope
and entered the level road.   Here Kitty and the
man started off at a canter, and I was left alone
with Mrs. Wessington.   "Agnes," said I, "will
you put back your hood and tell me what it all
means?"   The hood dropped noiselessly, and I was
face to face with my dead and buried mistress.
She was wearing the dress in which I had last
seen her alive; carried the same tiny handkerchief
in her right hand; and the same card-case in her
left.   (A woman eight months dead with a card-
case?)   I had to pin myself down to the multiplication-table, and to set both hands on the stone
parapet of the road, to assure myself that that
at least was real.

"Agnes," I repeated, "for pity's sake tell me what it all means." Mrs. Wessington leant forward with that odd, quick turn of the head I used to know so well, and spoke.

If my story had not already so madly overleaped the bounds of all human belief I should apologize to you now. As I know that no one—no, not even Kitty, for whom it is written as some sort of justification of my conduct—will believe me, I will go on. Mrs. Wessington spoke and I walked with her from the Sanjowlie road to the turning below the Commander-in-chief's house as I might walk by the side of any living woman's 'rickshaw, deep in conversation. The second and most tormenting of my moods of sickness had suddenly laid hold upon me, and like the Prince in Tennyson's poem, "I seemed to move amid a world of ghosts." There had been a garden-party at the Commander-in-chief's, and we two joined the crowd of homeward-bound folk. As I saw them then it seemed that they were the shadows—impalpable fantastic shadows—that divided for Mrs. Wessington's 'rickshaw to pass through. What we said during the course of that weird interview I cannot—indeed, I dare not—tell. Heatherlegh's comment would have been a short laugh and a remark that I had been "mashing a brain-eye-and-stomach chimera." It was a ghastly and yet in some indefinable way a marvelously dear experience. Could it be possible, I wondered, that I was in this life to woo a second time the woman I had killed by my own neglect and cruelty?

I met Kitty on the homeward road—a shadow among shadows.

If I were to describe all the incidents of the next fortnight in their order, my story would never come to an end; and your patience would be exhausted. Morning after morning and evening after evening the ghostly 'rickshaw and I used to wander through Simla together. Wherever I went there the four black and white liveries followed me and bore me company to and from my hotel. At the Theater I found them amid the crowd of yelling *jhampanies;* outside the Club veranda, after a long evening of whist; at the Birthday Ball, waiting patiently for my reappearance; and in broad daylight when I went calling. Save that it cast no shadow, the 'rickshaw was in every respect as real to look upon as one of wood and iron. More than once, indeed, I have had to check myself from warning some hardriding friend against cantering over it. More than once I have walked down the Mall deep in conversation with Mrs. Wessington to the unspeakable amazement of the passersby.

Before I had been out and about a week I learned that the "fit" theory had been discarded in favor of insanity. However, I made no change in my mode of life, I called, rode, and dined out as freely as ever. I had a passion for the society of my kind which I had never felt before; I hungered to be among the realities of life; and at the same time I felt vaguely unhappy when I had been separated too long from my ghostly companion. It would be almost impossible to describe my varying moods from the 15th of May up to to-day.

The presence of the 'rickshaw filled me by turns with horror, blind fear, a dim sort of pleasure, and utter despair. I dared not leave Simla; and I knew that my stay there was killing me. I knew, moreover, that it was my destiny to die slowly and a little every day. My only anxiety was to get the penance over as quietly as might be. Alternately I hungered for a sight of Kitty and watched her outrageous flirtations with my successor—to speak more accurately, my successors —with amused interest. She was as much out of my life as I was out of hers. By day I wandered with Mrs. Wessington almost content. By night I implored Heaven to let me return to the world as I used to know it. Above all these varying moods lay the sensation of dull, numbing wonder that the Seen and the Unseen should mingle so strangely on this earth to hound one poor soul to its grave.

．　　　．　　　．　　　．　　　．　　　．　　　．

August 27.—Heatherlegh has been indefatigable in his attendance on me; and only yesterday told me that I ought to send in an application for sick leave. An application to escape the company of a phantom! A request that the Government would graciously permit me to get rid of five ghosts and an airy 'rickshaw by going to England! Heatherlegh's proposition moved me almost to hysterical laughter. I told him that I should await the end quietly at Simla; and I am sure that the end is not far off. Believe me that I dread its advent more than any word can say; and I torture myself nightly with a thousand speculations as to the manner of my death.

Shall I die in my bed decently and as an English gentleman should die; or, in one last walk on the Mall, will my soul be wrenched from me to take its place forever and ever by the side of that ghastly phantasm? Shall I return to my old lost allegiance in the next world, or shall I meet Agnes, loathing her and bound to her side through all eternity? Shall we two hover over the scene of our lives till the end of Time? As the day of my death draws nearer, the intense horror that all living flesh feels towards escaped spirits from beyond the grave grows more and more powerful. It is an awful thing to go down quick among the dead with scarcely one-half of your life completed. It is a thousand times more awful to wait as I do in your midst, for I know not what unimaginable terror. Pity me, at least on the score of my "delusion," for I know you will never believe what I have written here. Yet as surely as ever a man was done to death by the Powers of Darkness I am that man.

In justice, too, pity her. For as surely as ever woman was killed by man, I killed Mrs. Wessington. And the last portion of my punishment is even now upon me.

THE STRANGE RIDE OF
MORROWBIE JUKES

THE STRANGE RIDE OF MORROWBIE JUKES

Alive or dead—there is no other way.—Native Proverb.

THERE is, as the conjurers say, no deception about this tale. Jukes by accident stumbled upon a village that is well known to exist, though he is the only Englishman who has been there. A somewhat similar institution used to flourish on the outskirts of Calcutta, and there is a story that if you go into the heart of Bikanir, which is in the heart of the Great Indian Desert, you shall come across not a village, but a town where the Dead who did not die but may not live have established their headquarters. And, since it is perfectly true that in the same Desert is a wonderful city where all the rich money-lenders retreat after they have made their fortunes (fortunes so vast that the owners cannot trust even the strong hand of the Government to protect them, but take refuge in the waterless sands), and drive sumptuous C-spring barouches, and buy beautiful girls and decorate their palaces with gold and ivory and Minton tiles and mother-o'-pearl, I do not see why Juke's tale should not be true. He is a Civil Engineer, with a head for plans and distances and things of that kind, and he certainly would not

45

take the trouble to invent imaginary traps. He could earn more by doing his legitimate work. He never varies the tale in the telling, and grows very hot and indignant when he thinks of the disrespectful treatment he received. He wrote this quite straightforwardly at first, but he has since touched it up in places and introduced Moral Reflections, thus:—

In the beginning it all arose from a slight attack of fever. My work necessitated my being in camp for some months between Pakpattan and Muba- rakpur—a desolate sandy stretch of country as every one who has had the misfortune to go there may know. My coolies were neither more nor less exasperating than other gangs, and my work demanded sufficient attention to keep me from moping, had I been inclined to do so unmanly a weakness.

On the 23rd December, 1884, I felt a little feverish. There was a full moon at the time, and, in consequence, every dog near my tent was bay- ing it. The brutes assembled in twos and threes and drove me frantic. A few days previously I had shot one loud-mouthed singer and suspended his carcass *in terrorem* about fifty yards from my tent-door. But his friends fell upon, fought for, and ultimately devoured the body: and, as it seemed to me, sang their hymns of thanksgiving afterwards with renewed energy.

The light-headedness which accompanies fever acts differently on different men. My irritation gave way, after a short time, to a fixed determination to slaughter one huge black and white beast who had been foremost in song and first in flight throughout the evening. Thanks to a shaking hand and a giddy head I had already missed him twice with both barrels of my shotgun, when it struck me that my best plan would be to ride him down in the open and finish him off with a hog-spear. This, of course, was merely the semi-delirious notion of a fever patient; but I remember that it struck me at the time as being eminently practical and feasible.

I therefore ordered my groom to saddle Pornic and bring him round quietly to the rear of my tent. When the pony was ready, I stood at his head and prepared to mount and dash out as soon as the dog should again lift up his voice. Pornic, by the way, had not been out of his pickets for a couple of days; the night air was crisp and chilly; and I was armed with a specially long and sharp pair of persuaders with which I had been rousing a sluggish cob that afternoon. You will easily believe, then, that when he was let go he went quickly. In one moment, for the brute bolted as straight as a die, the tent was left far behind, and we were flying over the smooth sandy soil at racing speed. In another we had passed the wretched dog, and I had almost forgotten why it was that I had taken horse and hog-spear.

The delirium of fever and the excitement of rapid motion through the air must have taken away the remnant of my senses. I have a faint recollection of standing upright in my stirrups, and of brandishing my hog-spear at the great white Moon that looked down so calmly on my mad gallop; and of shouting challenges to the camel-thorn bushes as they whizzed past. Once or twice, I believe, I swayed forward on Pornic's neck, and literally hung on by my spurs—as the marks next morning showed.

The wretched beast went forward like a thing possessed, over what seemed to be a limitless expanse of moonlit sand. Next, I remember, the ground rose suddenly in front of us, and as we topped the ascent I saw the waters of the Sutlej shining like a silver bar below. The Pornic blundered heavily on his nose, and we rolled together down some unseen slope.

I must have lost consciousness, for when I recovered I was lying on my stomach in a heap of soft white sand, and the dawn was beginning to break dimly over the edge of the slope down which I had fallen. As the light grew stronger I saw that I was at the bottom of a horseshoe-shaped crater of sand, opening on one side directly on to the shoals of the Sutlej. My fever had altogether left me, and with the exception of a slight dizziness in the head, I felt no bad effects from the fall over night.

Pornic, who was standing a few yards away, was naturally a good deal exhausted, but had not hurt himself in the least. His saddle, a favorite polo one, was much knocked about, and had been twisted under his belly. It took me some time to put him to rights, and in the meantime I had ample opportunities of observing the spot into which I had so foolishly dropped.

At the risk of being considered tedious, I must describe it at length; inasmuch as an accurate mental picture of its peculiarities will be of material assistance in enabling the reader to understand what follows.

Imagine then, as I have said before, a horseshoe-shaped crater of sand with steeply graded sand walls about thirty-five feet high. (The slope, I fancy, must have been about 65°). This crater enclosed a level piece of ground about fifty yards long by thirty at its broadest part, with a rude well in the center. Round the bottom of a crater, about three feet from the level of the ground proper, ran a series of eighty-three semi-circular, ovoid, square, and mutilateral holes, all about three feet at the mouth. Each hole on inspection showed that it was carefully shored internally with driftwood and bamboos, and over the mouth a wooden drip-board projected, like the peak of a jockey's cap, for two feet. No sign of life was visible in these tunnels, but a most sickening stench pervaded the entire amphitheater—a stench fouler than any which my wanderings in Indian villages have introduced me to.

Having remounted Pornic, who was as anxious as I to get back to camp, I rode round the base of the horseshoe to find some place whence an exit would be practicable. The inhabitants, whoever they might be, had not thought fit to put in an appearance, so I was left to my own devises. My first attempt to "rush" Pornic up the steep sandbanks showed me that I had fallen into a trap exactly on the same model as that which the ant-lion sets for its prey. At each step the shifting sand poured down from above in tons, and rattled on the drip-boards of the holes like small shot. A couple of ineffectual charges sent us both rolling down to the bottom, half choked with the torrents of sand; and I was constrained to turn my attention to the river-bank.

Here everything seemed easy enough. The sand hills ran down to the river edge, it is true, but there were plenty of shoals and shallows across which I could gallop Pornic, and find my way back to *terra firma* by turning sharply to the right or the left. As I led Pornic over the sands I was startled by the faint pop of a rifle across the river; and at the same moment a bullet dropped with a sharp "whit" close to Pornic's head.

There was no mistaking the nature of the missile—a regulation Martini-Henry "picket." About five hundred yards away a country-boat was anchored in midstream; and a jet of smoke drifting away from its bows in the still morning air showed me whence the delicate attention had come. Was ever a respectable gentleman in such an *impasse?* The treacherous sand slope allowed no escape from a spot which I had visited most involuntarily, and a promenade on the river frontage was the signal for a bombardment from some insane native in a boat. I'm afraid that I lost my temper very much indeed.

Another bullet reminded me that I had better save my breath to cool my porridge; and I retreated hastily up the sands and back to the horseshoe, where I saw that the noise of the rifle had drawn sixty-five human beings from the badgerholes which I had up till that point supposed to be untenanted. I found myself in the midst of a crowd of spectators—about forty men, twenty women, and one child who could not have been more than five years old. They were all scantily clothed in that salmon-colored cloth which one associates with Hindu mendicants, and, at first sight, gave me the impression of a band of loathsome *fakirs.* The filth and repulsiveness of the assembly were beyond all description, and I shuddered to think what their life in the badger-holes must be.

Even in these days, when local self-government has destroyed the greater part of a native's respect for a Sahib, I have been accustomed to a certain amount of civility from my inferiors, and on approaching the crowd naturally expected that there would be some recognition of my presence. As a matter of fact there was; but it was by no means what I had looked for.

The ragged crew actually laughed at me—such laughter I hope I may never hear again. They cackled, yelled, whistled, and howled as I walked into their midst; some of them literally throwing themselves down on the ground in convulsions of unholy mirth. In a moment I had let go Pornic's head, and, irritated beyond expression at the morning's adventure, commenced cuffing those nearest to me with all the force I could. The wretches dropped under my blows like nine-pins, and the laughter gave place to wails for mercy; while those yet untouched clasped me round the knees, imploring me in all sorts of uncouth tongues to spare them.

In the tumult, and just when I was feeling very much ashamed of myself for having thus easily given way to my temper, a thin, high voice murmured in English from behind my shoulder:— "Sahib! Sahib! Do you not know me? Sahib, it is Gunga Dass, the telegraph-master."

I spun round quickly and faced the speaker.

Gunga Dass (I have, of course, no hesitation in mentioning the man's real name) I had known four years before as a Deccanee Brahmin lent by the Punjab Government to one of the Khalsia States. He was in charge of a branch telegraph-office there, and when I had last met him was a jovial, full-stomached, portly Government serv-ant with a marvelous capacity for making bad

puns in English—a peculiarity which made me remember him long after I had forgotten his services to me in his official capacity. It is seldom
that a Hindu makes English puns.

Now, however, the man was changed beyond all
recognition. Caste-mark, stomach, state-colored
continuations, and unctuous speech were all gone.
I looked at a withered skeleton, turbanless and
almost naked, with long matted hair and deep-set
codfish-eyes. But for a crescent-shaped scar on
the left cheek—the result of an accident for which
I was responsible—I should never have known
him. But it was indubitably Gunga Dass, and—
for this I was thankful—an English-speaking native who might at least tell me the meaning of all
that I had gone through that day.

The crowd retreated to some distance as I
turned towards the miserable figure, and ordered
him to show me some method of escaping from the
crater. He held a freshly-plucked crow in his
hand, and in reply to my question climbed slowly
on a platform of sand which ran in front of the
holes, and commenced lighting a fire there in silence. Dried bents, sand-poppies, and driftwood
burn quickly; and I derived much consolation from
the fact that he lit them with an ordinary sulphur-
match. When they were in a bright glow, and the
crow was neatly spitted in front thereof, Gunga
Dass began without a word of preamble:—

"There are only two kinds of men, Sar. The
alive and the dead. When you are dead you are

dead, but when you are alive you live." (Here the crow demanded his attention for an instant as it twirled before the fire in danger of being burnt to a cinder.) "If you die at home and do not die when you come to the ghât to be burnt you come here."

The nature of the reeking village was made plain now, and all that I had known or read of the grotesque and the horrible paled before the fact just communicated by the ex-Brahmin. Sixteen years ago, when I first landed in Bombay, I had been told by a wandering Armenian of the existence, somewhere in India, of a place to which such Hindus as had the misfortune to recover from trance or catalepsy were conveyed and kept, and I recollect laughing heartily at what I was then pleased to consider a traveler's tale. Sitting at the bottom of the sand-trap, the memory of Watson's Hotel, with its swinging punkahs, white-robed attendants, and the sallowed faced Armenian, rose up in my mind as vividly as a photograph, and I burst into a loud fit of laughter. The contrast was too absurd!

Gunga Dass, as he bent over the unclean bird, watched me curiously. Hindus seldom laugh, and his surroundings were not such as to move Gunga Dass to any undue excess of hilarity. He removed the crow solemnly from the wooden spit and as solemnly devoured it. Then he continued his story, which I give in his own words:—

"In epidemics of the cholera you are carried

to be burnt almost before you are dead. When you come to the riverside the cold air, perhaps, makes you alive, and then, if you are only little alive, mud is put on your nose and mouth and you die conclusively. If you are rather more alive, more mud is put; but if you are too lively they let you go and take you away. I was too lively, and made protestation with anger against the indignities that they endeavored to press upon me. In those days I was Brahmin and proud man. Now I am dead man and eat"—here he eyed the well-gnawed breast bone with the first sign of emotion that I had seen in him since we met—"crows, and other things. They took me from my sheets when they saw that I was too lively and gave me medicines for one week, and I survived successfully. Then they sent me by rail from my place to Okara Station with a man to take care of me; and at Okara Station we met two other men, and they conducted we three on camels, in the night, from Okara Station to this place, and they propelled me from the top to the bottom, and the other two succeeded, and I have been here ever since, two and a half years. Once I was Brahmin and proud man, and now I eat crows."

"There is no way of getting out?"

"None of what kind at all. When I first came I made experiments frequently and all the others also, but we have always succumbed to the sand which is precipitated upon our heads."

"But surely," I broke in at this point, "the

river-front is open, and it is worth while dodging
the bullets; while at night——"

I had already matured a rough plan of escape
which a natural instinct of selfishness forbade me
sharing with Gunga Dass. He, however, di-
vined my unspoken thought almost as soon as it
was formed; and, to my intense astonishment,
gave vent to a long low chuckle of derision—the
laughter, be it understood, of a superior or at least
of an equal. "You will not"—he had dropped the
Sir completely after his opening sentence—"make
any escape that way. But you can try. I have
tried. Once only."

The sensation of nameless terror and abject
fear which I had in vain attempted to strive
against overmastered me completely. My long
fast—it was now close upon ten o'clock, and I had
eaten nothing since tiffin on the previous day—
combined with the violent and unnatural agita-
tion of the ride had exhausted me, and I verily
believe that, for a few minutes, I acted as one
mad. I hurled myself against the pitiless sand-
slope. I ran round the base of the crater, blas-
pheming and praying by turns. I crawled out
among the sedges of the river-front, only to be
driven back each time in an agony of nervous
dread by the rifle-bullets which cut up the sand
round me—for I dared not face the death of a mad
dog among that hideous crowd—and finally fell,
spent and raving, at the curb of the well. No
one had taken the slightest notice of an exhibition

which makes me blush hotly even when I think of it now.

Two or three men trod on my panting body as they drew water, but they were evidently used to this sort of thing, and had no time to waste upon me. The situation was humiliating. Gunga Dass, indeed, when he had banked the embers of his fire with sand, was at some pains to throw half a cupful of fetid water over my head, an attention for which I could have fallen on my knees and thanked him, but he was laughing all the while in the same mirthless, wheezy key that greeted me on my first attempt to force the shoals. And so, in a semi-comatose condition, I lay till noon. Then, being only a man after all, I felt hungry, and intimated as much to Gunga Dass, whom I had begun to regard as my natural protector. Following the impulse of the outer world when dealing with natives, I put my hand into my pocket and drew out four annas. The absurdity of the gift struck me at once, and I was about to replace the money.

Gunga Dass, however, was of a different opinion. "Give me the money," said he; "all you have, or I will get help, and we will kill you!" All this as if it were the most natural thing in the world!

A Briton's first impulse, I believe, is to guard the contents of his pockets; but a moment's reflection convinced me of the futility of differing with the one man who had it in his power to make me comfortable; and with whose help it was possible that I might eventually escape from the crater. I gave him all the money in my possession, Rs. 9-8-5—nine rupees eight annas and five pie—for I always keep small change as *bakshish* when I am in camp. Gunga Dass clutched the coins, and hid them at once in his ragged loincloth, his expression changing to something diabolical as he looked round to assure himself that no one had observed us.

"Now I will give you something to eat," said he.

What pleasure the possession of my money could have afforded him I am unable to say; but inasmuch as it did give him evident delight I was not sorry that I had parted with it so readily, for I had no doubt that he would have had me killed if I had refused. One does not protest against the vagaries of a den of wild beasts; and my companions were lower than any beasts. While I devoured what Gunga Dass had provided, a coarse *chapatti* and a cupful of the foul well-water, the people showed not the faintest sign of curiosity—that curiosity which is so rampant, as a rule, in an Indian village.

I could even fancy that they despised me. At all events they treated me with the most chilling indifference, and Gunga Dass was nearly as bad. I plied him with questions about the terrible village, and received extremely unsatisfactory answers. So far as I could gather, it had been in existence from time immemorial—whence I concluded that it was at least a century old—and during that time no one had ever been known to escape from it. (I had to control myself here with both hands, lest the blind terror should lay hold of me a second time and drive me raving round the crater.) Gunga Dass took a malicious pleasure in emphasizing this point and in watching me wince. Nothing that I could do would induce him to tell me who the mysterious "They" were.

"It is so ordered," he would reply, "and I do not yet know one who has disobeyed the orders."

"Only wait till my servants find that I am missing," I retorted, "and I promise you that this place shall be cleared off the face of the earth, and I'll give you a lesson in civility, too, my friend."

"Your servants would be torn in pieces before they came near this place; and, besides, you are dead, my dear friend. It is not your fault, of course, but none the less you are dead and buried."

At irregular intervals supplies of food, I was told, were dropped down from the land side into the amphitheater, and the inhabitants fought for them like wild beasts. When a man felt his death coming on he retreated to his lair and died there. The body was sometimes dragged out of the hole and thrown on to the sand, or allowed to rot where it lay.

The phrase "thrown on to the sand" caught my attention, and I asked Gunga Dass whether this sort of thing was not likely to breed a pestilence.

"That," said he, with another of his wheezy chuckles, "you may see for yourself subsequently. You will have much time to make observations."

Whereat, to his great delight, I winced once more and hastily continued the conversation:— "And how do you live here from day to day? What do you do?" The question elicited exactly the same answer as before—coupled with the information that "this place is like your European heaven; there is neither marrying nor giving in marriage."

Gunga Dass had been educated at a Mission School, and, as he himself admitted, had he only changed his religion "like a wise man," might have avoided the living grave which was now his portion. But as long as I was with him I fancy he was happy.

Here was a Sahib, a representative of the dominant race, helpless as a child and completely at the mercy of his native neighbors. In a deliberate lazy way he set himself to torture me as a schoolboy would devote a rapturous half-hour to watching the agonies of an impaled beetle, or as a ferret in a blind burrow might glue himself comfortably to the neck of a rabbit. The burden of his conversation was that there was no escape "of no kind whatever," and that I should stay here till I died and was "thrown on to the sand." If it were possible to forejudge the conversation of the Damned on the advent of a new soul in their abode, I should say that they would speak as

Gunga Dass did to me throughout that long afternoon. I was powerless to protest or answer; all
my energies being devoted to a struggle against
the inexplicable terror that threatened to over-
whelm me again and again. I can compare the
feeling to nothing except the struggles of a man
against the overpowering nausea of the Channel
passage—only my agony was of the spirit and in-
finitely more terrible.

As the day wore on, the inhabitants began to
appear in full strength to catch the rays of the
afternoon sun, which were now sloping in at the
mouth of the crater. They assembled in little
knots, and talked among themselves without even
throwing a glance in my direction. About four
o'clock, as far as I could judge, Gunga Dass rose
and dived into his lair for a moment, emerging
with a live crow in his hands. The wretched bird
was in a most draggled and deplorable condition,
but seemed to be in no way afraid of its master.
Advancing cautiously to the river-front, Gunga
Dass stepped from tussock to tussock until he had
reached a smooth patch of sand directly in the
line of the boat's fire. The occupants of the boat
took no notice. Here he stopped, and with a
couple of dexterous turns of the wrist, pegged the
bird on its back with outstretched wings. As was
only natural, the crow began to shriek at once and
beat the air with its claws. In a few seconds the
clamor had attracted the attention of a bevy of
wild crows on a shoal a few hundred yards away,

where they were discussing something that looked like a corpse. Half a dozen crows flew over at once to see what was going on, and also, as it proved, to attack the pinioned bird. Gunga Dass, who had lain down on a tussock, motioned to me to be quiet, though I fancy this was a needless precaution. In a moment, and before I could see how it happened, a wild crow, who had grappled with the shrieking and helpless bird, was entangled in the latter's claws, swiftly disengaged by Gunga Dass, and pegged down beside its companion in adversity. Curiosity, it seemed, overpowered the rest of the flock, and almost before Gunga Dass and I had time to withdraw to the tussock, two more captives were struggling in the upturned claws of the decoys. So the chase—if I can give it so dignified a name—continued until Gunga Dass had captured seven crows. Five of them he throttled at once, reserving two for further operations another day. I was a good deal impressed by this, to me, novel method of securing food, and complimented Gunga Dass on his skill.

"It is nothing to do," said he. "To-morrow you must do it for me. You are stronger than I am."

This calm assumption of superiority upset me not a little, and I answered peremptorily:—"Indeed, you old ruffian! What do you think I have given you money for?"

"Very well," was the unmoved reply. "Per-

haps not to-morrow, nor the day after, nor subsequently; but in the end, and for many years, you
will catch crows and eat crows, and you will thank
your European Gods that you have crows to catch
and eat."

I could have cheerfully strangled him for this;
but judged it best under the circumstances to
smother my resentment. An hour later I was eating one of the crows; and, as Gunga Dass had
said, thanking my God that I had a crow to eat.
Never as long as I live shall I forget that evening
meal. The whole population were squatting on
the hard sand platform opposite their dens, hud-
dled over tiny fires of refuse and dried rushes.
Death, having once laid his hand upon these men
and forborne to strike, seemed to stand aloof from
them now; for most of our company were old
men, bent and worn and twisted with years, and
women aged to all appearance as the Fates themselves. They sat together in knots and talked—
God only knows what they found to discuss—in
low equable tones, curious in contrast to the
strident babble with which natives are accustomed
to make day hideous. Now and then an access of
that sudden fury which had possessed me in the
morning would lay hold on a man or woman;
and with yells and imprecations the sufferer would
attack the steep slope until, baffled and bleeding,
he fell back on the platform incapable of moving
a limb. The others would never even raise their
eyes when this happened, as men too well aware

of the futility of their fellows' attempts and wearied with their useless repetition. I saw four such outbursts in the course of that evening.

Gunga Dass took an eminently business-like view of my situation, and while we were dining—I can afford to laugh at the recollection now, but it was painful enough at the time—propounded the terms on which he would consent to "do" for me. My nine rupees eight annas, he argued, at the rate of three annas a day, would provide me with food for fifty-one days, or about seven weeks; that is to say, he would be willing to cater for me for that length of time. At the end of it I was to look after myself. For a further consideration—*videlicet* my boots—he would be willing to allow me to occupy the den next to his own, and would supply me with as much dried grass for bedding as he could spare.

"Very well, Gunga Dass," I replied; "to the first terms I cheerfully agree, but as there is nothing on earth to prevent my killing you as you sit here and taking everything that you have" (I thought of the two invaluable crows at the time), "I flatly refuse to give you my boots and shall take whichever den I please."

The stroke was a bold one, and I was glad when I saw that it had succeeded. Gunga Dass changed his tone immediately, and disavowed all intention of asking for my boots. At the time it did not strike me as at all strange that I, a Civil Engineer, a man of thirteen years' stand-

ing in the Service, and I trust, an average Englishman, should thus calmly threaten murder and
violence against the man who had, for a consideration, it is true, taken me under his wing. I had
left the world, it seemed, for centuries. I was
as certain then as I am now of my own existence,
that in the accursed settlement there was no law
save that of the strongest; that the living dead
men had thrown behind them every canon of the
world which had cast them out; and that I had to
depend for my own life on my strength and
vigilance alone. The crew of the ill-fated Mig-
nonette are the only men who would understand
my frame of mind. "At present," I argued to
myself, "I am strong and a match for six of these
wretches. It is imperatively necessary that I
should, for my own sake, keep both health and
strength until the hour of my release comes—if
it ever does."

Fortified with these resolutions, I ate and drank
as much as I could, and made Gunga Dass understand that I intended to be his master, and that
the least sign of insubordination on his part would
be visited with the only punishment I had it in
my power to inflict—sudden and violent death.
Shortly after this I went to bed. That is to say,
Gunga Dass gave me a double armful of dried
bents which I thrust down the mouth of the lair
to the right of his, and followed myself, feet foremost; the hole running about nine feet into the
sand with a slight downward inclination, and

being neatly shored with timbers.   From my den, which faced the river-front, I was able to watch the waters of the Sutlej flowing past under the light of a young moon and composed myself to sleep as best I might.

The horrors of that night I shall never forget. My den was nearly as narrow as a coffin, and the sides had been worn smooth and greasy by the contact of innumerable naked bodies, added to which it smelled abominably.   Sleep was altogether out of question to one in my excited frame of mind.   As the night wore on, it seemed that the entire amphitheater was filled with legions of unclean devils that, trooping up from the shoals below, mocked the unfortunates in their lairs.

Personally I am not of an imaginative temperament,—very few Engineers are,—but on that occasion I was as completely prostrated with nervous terror as any woman.   After half an hour or so, however, I was able once more to calmly review my chances of escape.   Any exit by the steep sand walls was, of course, impracticable. I had been thoroughly convinced of this some time before.   It was possible, just possible, that I might, in the uncertain moonlight, safely run the gauntlet of the rifle shots.   The place was so full of terror for me that I was prepared to undergo any risk in leaving it.   Imagine my delight, then, when after creeping stealthily to the river-front I found that the infernal boat was not there.   My freedom lay before me in the next few steps!

By walking out to the first shallow pool that lay at the foot of the projecting left horn of the horseshoe, I could wade across, turn the flank of the crater, and make my way inland. Without a moment's hesitation I marched briskly past the tussocks where Gunga Dass had snared the crows, and out in the direction of the smooth white sand beyond. My first step from the tufts of dried grass showed me how utterly futile was any hope of escape; for, as I put my foot down, I felt an indescribable drawing, sucking motion of the sand below. Another moment and my leg was swallowed up nearly to the knee. In the moonlight the whole surface of the sand seemed to be shaken with devilish delight at my disappointment. I struggled clear, sweating with terror and exertion, back to the tussocks behind me and fell on my face.

My only means of escape from the semi-circle was protected with a quicksand!

How long I lay I have not the faintest idea; but I was roused at last by the malevolent chuckle of Gunga Dass at my ear. "I would advise you, Protector of the Poor (the ruffian was speaking English) "to return to your house. It is unhealthy to lie down here. Moreover, when the boat returns, you will most certainly be rifled at." He stood over me in the dim light of the dawn, chuckling and laughing to himself. Suppressing my first impulse to catch the man by the neck and throw him on the quicksand, I rose sullenly and followed him to the platform below the burrows.

Suddenly, and futilely as I thought while I spoke, I asked:—"Gunga Dass, what is the good of the boat if I can't get out anyhow?" I recollect that even in my deepest trouble I had been speculating vaguely on the waste of ammunition in guarding an already well protected foreshore.

Gunga Dass laughed again and made answer:— "They have the boat only in daytime. It is for the reason that there is a way. I hope we shall have the pleasure of your company for much longer time. It is a pleasant spot when you have been here some years and eaten roast crow long enough."

I staggered, numbed and helpless, towards the fetid burrow allotted to me, and fell asleep. An hour or so later I was awakened by a piercing scream—the shrill, high-pitched scream of a horse in pain. Those who have once heard that will never forget the sound. I found some little difficulty in scrambling out of the burrow. When I was in the open, I saw Pornic, my poor old Pornic, lying dead on the sandy soil. How they had killed him I cannot guess. Gunga Dass explained that horse was better than crow, and "greatest good of greatest number," is political maxim. We are now Republic, Mister Jukes, and you are entitled to a fair share of the beast. If you like, we will pass a vote of thanks. Shall I propose?"

Yes, we were a Republic indeed! A Republic

of wild beasts penned at the bottom of a pit, to eat and fight and sleep till we died. I attempted no protest of any kind, but sat down and stared at the hideous sight in front of me. In less time than it takes me to write this, Pornic's body was divided, in some unclean way or other; the men and women had dragged the fragments on to the platform and were preparing their morning meal. Gunga Dass cooked mine. The almost irresistible impulse to fly at the sand walls until I was wearied laid hold of me afresh, and I had to struggle against it with all my might. Gunga Dass was offensively jocular till I told him that if he addressed another remark of any kind whatever to me I should strangle him where he sat. This silenced him till silence became insupportable, and I bade him say something.

"You will live here till you die like the other Feringhi," he said coolly, watching me over the fragment of gristle that he was gnawing.

"What other Sahib, you swine? Speak at once, and don't stop to tell me a lie."

"He is over there," answered Gunga Dass, pointing to a burrow-mouth about four doors to the left of my own. "You can see for yourself. He died in the burrow as you will die, and I will die, and as all these men and women and the one child will also die."

"For pity's sake tell me all you know about him. Who was he? When did he come, and when did he die?"

This appeal was a weak step on my part. Gunga Dass only leered and replied:—"I will not —unless you give me something first."

Then I recollected where I was, and struck the man between the eyes, partially stunning him. He stepped down from the platform at once, and, cringing and fawning and weeping and attempting to embrace my feet, led me round to the burrow which he had indicated.

"I know nothing whatever about the gentleman. Your God be my witness that I do not. He was as anxious to escape as you were, and he was shot from the boat, though we all did all things to prevent him from attempting. He was shot here." Gunga Dass laid his hand on his lean stomach and bowed to the earth.

"Well, and what then? Go on!"

"And then—and then, Your Honor, we carried him in to his house and gave him water, and put wet cloths on the wound, and he laid down in his house and gave up the ghost."

"In how long? In how long?"

"About half an hour, after he received his wound. I call Vishn to witness," yelled the wretched man, "that I did everything for him. Everything which was possible, that I did!"

He threw himself down on the ground and clasped my ankles. But I had my doubts about Gunga Dass's benevolence, and kicked him off as he lay protesting.

"I believe you robbed him of everything he

had. But I can find out in a minute or two. How long was the Sahib here?"

"Nearly a year and a half. I think he must have gone mad. But hear me swear, Protector of the Poor! Won't Your Honor hear me swear that I never touched an article that belonged to him? What is Your Worship going to do?"

I had taken Gunga Dass by the waist and had hauled him on to the platform opposite the deserted burrow. As I did so I thought of my wretched fellow-prisoner's unspeakable misery among all these horrors for eighteen months, and the final agony of dying like a rat in a hole, with a bullet-wound in the stomach. Gunga Dass fancied I was going to kill him and howled pitifully. The rest of the population, in the plethora that follows a full flesh meal, watched us without stirring.

"Go inside, Gunga Dass," said I, "and fetch it out."

I was feeling sick and faint with horror now. Gunga Dass nearly rolled off the platform and howled aloud.

"But I am a Brahmin, Sahib—a high-caste Brahmin. By your soul, by your father's soul, do not make me do this thing!"

"Brahmin or no Brahmin, by my soul and my father's soul, in you go!" I said, and, seizing him by the shoulders, I crammed his head into the mouth of the burrow, kicked the rest of him in, and, sitting down, covered my face with my hands.

At the end of a few minutes I heard a rustle and a creak; then Gunga Dass in a sobbing, choking whisper speaking to himself; then a soft thud —and I uncovered my eyes.

The dry sand had turned the corpse entrusted to its keeping into a yellow-brown mummy. I told Gunga Dass to stand off while I examined it. The body—clad in an olive-green hunting-suit much stained and worn, with leather pads on the shoulders—was that of a man between thirty and forty, above middle height, with light, sandy hair, long mustache, and a rough unkempt beard. The left canine of the upper jaw was missing, and a portion of the lobe of the right ear was gone. On the second finger of the left hand was a ring—a shield-shaped bloodstone set in gold, with a monogram that might have been either "B. K." or "B. L." On the third finger of the right hand was a silver ring in the shape of a coiled cobra, much worn and tarnished. Gunga Dass deposited a handful of trifles he had picked out of the burrow at my feet, and, covering the face of the body with my handkerchief, I turned to examine these. I give the full list in the hope that it may lead to the identification of the unfortunate man:—

1. Bowl of a briarwood pipe, serrated at the edge; much worn and blackened; bound with string at the screw.

2.   Two patent-lever keys; wards of both broken.

3.   Tortoise-shell handled penknife, silver or nickel, name-plate, marked with monogram "B. K."

4.   Envelope, post-mark undecipherable, bearing a Victorian stamp, addressed to "Miss Mon—" (rest illegible)—"ham"—"nt."

5.   Imitation crocodile-skin note-book with pencil. First forty-five pages blank; four and a half illegible; fifteen others filled with private memoranda relating chiefly to three persons—a Mrs. L. Singleton, abbreviated several times to "Lot Single," "Mrs. S. May," and "Garmison," referred to in places as "Jerry" or "Jack."

6.   Handle of small-sized hunting-knife. Blade snapped short. Buck's horn, diamond cut, with swivel and ring on the butt; fragment of cotton cord attached.

It must not be supposed that I inventoried all these things on the spot as fully as I have here written them down. The note-book first attracted my attention, and I put it in my pocket with a view of studying it later on. The rest of the articles I conveyed to my burrow for safety's sake, and there being a methodical man, I inventoried them. I then returned to the corpse and ordered Gunga Dass to help me to carry it out to the river-front. While we were engaged in this, the exploded shell of an old brown cartridge dropped out of one of the pockets and rolled at my feet.   Gunga Dass had not seen it; and I fell to thinking that a man does not carry exploded cartridge-cases, especially "browns," which will not bear loading twice, about with him when shooting. In other words, that cartridge-case had been fired inside the crater. Consequently there must be a gun somewhere. I was on the verge of asking Gunga Dass, but checked myself, knowing that he would lie. We laid the body down on the edge of the quicksand by the tussocks. It was my intention to push it out and let it be swallowed up—the only possible mode of burial that I could think of. I ordered Gunga Dass to go away.

Then I gingerly put the corpse out on the quicksand. In doing so, it was lying face downward, I tore the frail and rotten khaki shooting-coat open, disclosing a hideous cavity in the back. I have already told you that the dry sand had, as it were, mummified the body. A moment's glance showed that the gaping hole had been caused by a gun-shot wound; the gun must have been fired with the muzzle almost touching the back. The shooting-coat, being intact, had been drawn over the body after death, which must have been instantaneous. The secret of the poor wretch's death was plain to me in a flash. Some one of the crater, presumably Gunga Dass, must have shot him with his own gun—the gun that fitted the brown cartridges. He had never attempted to escape in the face of the rifle-fire from the boat.

I pushed the corpse out hastily, and saw it sink from sight literally in a few seconds. I shuddered as I watched. In a dazed, half-conscious way I turned to peruse the notebook. A stained and discolored slip of paper had been inserted between the binding and the back, and dropped out as I opened the pages. This is what it contained:—
"Four out from crow-clump: three left; nine out; two right; three back; two left; fourteen out; two left; seven out; one left; nine back; two right; six back; four right; seven back." The paper had been burnt and charred at the edges. What it meant I could not understand. I sat down on the dried bents turning it over and over between my fingers, until I was aware of Gunga Dass standing immediately behind me with glowing eyes and outstretched hands.

"Have you got it?" he panted. "Will you not let me look at it also? I swear that I will return it."

"Got what? Return what?" I asked.

"That which you have in your hands. It will help us both." He stretched out his long, bird-like talons, trembling with eagerness.

"I could never find it," he continued. "He had secreted it about his person. Therefore I shot him, but nevertheless I was unable to obtain it."

Gunga Dass had quite forgotten his little fiction about the rifle-bullet. I received the information perfectly calmly. Morality is blunted by consorting with the Dead who are alive.

"What on earth are you raving about? What is it you want me to give you?"

"The piece of paper in the note-book. It will help us both. Oh, you fool! You fool! Can you not see what it will do for us? We shall escape!"

His voice rose almost to a scream, and he danced with excitement before me. I own I was moved at the chance of getting away.

"Don't skip! Explain yourself. Do you mean to say that this slip of paper will help us? What does it mean?"

"Read it aloud! Read it aloud! I beg and I pray to you to read it aloud."

I did so. Gunga Dass listened delightedly, and drew an irregular line in the sand with his fingers.

"See now! It was the length of his gun-barrels without the stock. I have those barrels. Four gun-barrels out from the place where I caught crows. Straight out; do you follow me? Then three left—Ah! how well I remember when that man worked it out night after night. Then nine out, and so on. Out is always straight before you across the quicksand. He told me so before I killed him."

"But if you knew all this why didn't you get out before?"

"I did not know it. He told me that he was working it out a year and a half ago, and how he was working it out night after night when the boat had gone away, and he could get out near the quicksand safely. Then he said that we would get away together. But I was afraid that he would leave me behind one night when he had worked it all out, and so I shot him. Besides, it is not advisable that the men who once get in here should escape. Only I, and I am Brahmin."

The prospect of escape had brought Gunga Dass's caste back to him. He stood up, walked about and gesticulated violently. Eventually I managed to make him talk soberly, and he told me how this Englishman had spent six months night after night in exploring, inch by inch, the passage across the quicksand; how he had declared it to be simplicity itself up to within about twenty yards of the river bank after turning the flank of the left horn of the horseshoe. This much he had evidently not completed when Gunga Dass shot him with his own gun.

In my frenzy of delight at the possibilities of escape I recollect shaking hands effusively with Gunga Dass, after we had decided that we were to make an attempt to get away that very night. It was weary work waiting throughout the afternoon.

About ten o'clock, as far as I could judge, when the Moon had just risen above the lip of the crater, Gunga Dass made a move for his burrow to bring out the gun-barrels whereby to measure our path. All the other wretched inhabitants had retired to their lairs long ago. The guardian boat drifted downstream some hours before, and we were utterly alone by the crow-clump. Gunga

Dass, while carrying the gun-barrels, let slip the piece of paper which was to be our guide. I stooped down hastily to recover it, and, as I did so, I was aware that the diabolical Brahmin was aiming a violent blow at the back of my head with the gun-barrels. It was too late to turn round. I must have received the blow somewhere on the nape of my neck. A hundred thousand fiery stars danced before my eyes, and I fell forward senseless at the edge of the quicksand.

When I recovered consciousness, the Moon was going down, and I was sensible of intolerable pain in the back of my head. Gunga Dass had disappeared and my mouth was full of blood. I lay down again and prayed that I might die without more ado. Then the unreasoning fury which I have before mentioned laid hold upon me, and I staggered inland towards the walls of the crater. It seemed that some one was calling to me in a whisper—"Sahib! Sahib! Sahib!" exactly as my bearer used to call me in the mornings. I fancied that I was delirious until a handful of sand fell at my feet. Then I looked up and saw a head peering down into the amphitheater—the head of Dunnoo, my dog-boy, who attended to my collies. As soon as he had attracted my attention, he held up his hand and showed a rope. I motioned, staggering to and fro the while, that he should throw it down. It was a couple of leather punkah-ropes knotted together, with a loop at one end. I slipped the loop over my head and under my arms; heard Dunnoo urge something forward; was conscious that I was being dragged, face downward, up the steep sand slope, and the next instant found myself choked and half fainting on the sand hills overlooking the crater. Dunnoo, with his face ashy gray in the moonlight, implored me not to stay but to get back to my tent at once.

It seems that he had tracked Pornic's footprints fourteen miles across the sands to the crater; had returned and told my servants, who flatly refused to meddle with any one, white or black, once fallen into the hideous Village of the Dead; whereupon Dunnoo had taken one of my ponies and a couple of punkah ropes, returned to the crater, and hauled me out as I have described.

To cut a long story short, Dunnoo is now my personal servant on a gold mohur a month—a sum which I still think far too little for the services he has rendered. Nothing on earth will induce me to go near that devilish spot again, or to reveal its whereabouts more clearly than I have done. Of Gunga Dass I have never found a trace, nor do I wish to do. My sole motive in giving this to be published is the hope that some one may possibly identify, from the details and the inventory which I have given above, the corpse of the man in the olive-green hunting-suit.

THE RECRUDESCENCE
OF IMRAY

THE RECRUDESCENCE OF IMRAY

IMRAY had achieved the impossible. Without warning, for no conceivable motive, in his youth and at the threshold of his career he had chosen to disappear from the world—which is to say, the little Indian station where he lived. Upon a day he was alive, well, happy, and in great evidence at his club, among the billiard-tables. Upon a morning he was not, and no manner of search could make sure where he might be. He had stepped out of his place; he had not appeared at his office at the proper time, and his dog-cart was not upon the public roads. For these reasons and because he was hampering in a microscopical degree the admiration of the Indian Empire, the Indian Empire paused for one microscopical moment to make inquiry into the fate of Imray. Ponds were dragged, wells were plumbed, telegrams were dispatched down the lines of railways and to the nearest seaport town—1,200 miles away—but Imray was not at the end of the drag-ropes nor the telegrams. He was gone, and his place knew him no more. Then the work of the great Indian Empire swept forward, because it could not be delayed, and Imray, from being a man, became a mystery—such a thing as men talk over at their tables in the club for a month and then forget utterly. His guns, horses, and carts were sold to the highest bidder. His superior office wrote an absurd letter to his mother, saying that Imray had unaccountably disappeared and his bungalow stood empty on the road.

After three or four months of the scorching hot weather had gone by, my friend Strickland, of the police force, saw fit to rent the bungalow from the native landlord. This was before he was engaged to Miss Youghai—an affair which has been described in another place—and while he was pursuing his investigations into native life. His own life was sufficiently peculiar, and men complained of his manners and customs. There was always food in his house, but there were no regular times for meals. He ate, standing up and walking about, whatever he might find on the side-board, and this is not good for the insides of human beings. His domestic equipment was limited to six rifles, three shotguns, five saddles, and a collection of stiff-jointed masheer rods, bigger and stronger than the largest salmon rods. These things occupied one-half of his bungalow, and the other half was given up to Strickland and his dog Tietjens—an enormous Rampur slut, who sung when she was ordered, and devoured daily the rations of two men. She spoke to Strickland in a language of her own, and whenever in her walks abroad she saw things calculated to destroy the peace of Her Majesty the Queen Empress, she returned to her master and gave him information. Strickland would take steps at once, and the end of his labors was trouble and fine and imprisonment for other people. The natives believed that Tietjens was a familiar spirit, and treated her with the great reverence that is born of hate and fear. One room in the bungalow was set apart for her special use. She owned a bedstead, a blanket, and a drinking-trough, and if any one came into Strickland's room at night, her custom was to knock down the invader and give tongue till some one came with a light. Strickland owes his life to her. When he was on the frontier in search of the local murderer who came in the gray dawn to send Strickland much further than the Andaman Islands, Tietjens caught him as he was crawling into Strickland's tent with a dagger between his teeth, and after his record of iniquity was established in the eyes of the law, he was hanged. From that date Tietjens wore a collar of rough silver and employed a monogram on her night blanket, and the blanket was double-woven Kashmir cloth, for she was a delicate dog.

Under no circumstances would she be separated from Strickland, and when he was ill with fever she made great trouble for the doctors because she did not know how to help her master and would not allow another creature to attempt aid. Macarnaght, of the Indian Medical Service, beat her over the head with a gun, before she could understand that she must give room for those who could give quinine.

A short time after Strickland had taken Imray's bungalow, my business took me through that station, and naturally, the club quarters being full, I quartered myself upon Strickland. It was a desirable bungalow, eight-roomed, and heavily thatched against any chance of leakage from rain. Under the pitch of the roof ran a ceiling cloth, which looked just as nice as a white-washed ceiling. The landlord had repainted it when Strickland took the bungalow, and unless you knew how Indian bungalows were built you would never have suspected that above the cloth lay the dark, three-cornered cavern of the roof, where the beams and the under side of the thatch harbored all manner of rats, bats, ants, and other things.

Tietjens met me in the veranda with a bay like the boom of the bells of St. Paul's, and put her paws on my shoulders and said she was glad to see me. Strickland had contrived to put together that sort of meal which he called lunch, and immediately after it was finished went out about his business. I was left alone with Tietjens and my own affairs. The heat of the summer had broken up and given place to the warm damp of the rains. There was no motion in the heated air, but the rain fell like bayonet rods on the earth, and flung up a blue mist where it splashed back again. The bamboos and the custard apples, the poinsettias and the mango-trees in the garden stood still while the warm water lashed through them, and the frogs began to sing among the aloe hedges. A little before the light failed, and when the rain was at its worst, I sat in the back veranda and heard the water roar from the eaves, and scratched myself because I was covered with the thing they call prickly heat. Tietjens came out with me and put her head in my lap, and was very sorrowful, so I gave her biscuits when tea was ready, and I took tea in the back veranda on account of the little coolness I found there. The rooms of the house were dark behind me. I could smell Strickland's saddlery and the oil on his guns, and I did not the least desire to sit among these things. My own servant came to me in the twilight, the muslin of his clothes clinging tightly to his drenched body, and told me that a gentleman had called and wished to see some one. Very much against my will, and because of the darkness of the rooms, I went into the naked drawing-room, telling my man to bring the lights. There might or might not have been a caller in the room —it seems to me that I saw a figure by one of the windows, but when the lights came there was nothing save the spikes of the rain without and the smell of the drinking earth in my nostrils. I explained to my man that he was no wiser than he ought to be, and went back to the veranda to talk to Tietjens. She had gone out into the wet and I could hardly coax her back to me—even with biscuits with sugar on top. Strickland rode back, dripping wet, just before dinner, and the first thing he said was:

"Has any one called?"

I explained, with apologies, that my servant had called me into the drawing-room on a false alarm; or that some loafer had tried to call on Strickland, and, thinking better of it, fled after giving his name. Strickland ordered dinner without comment and since it was a real dinner, with white table-cloth attached, we sat down.

At nine o'clock Strickland wanted to go to bed, and I was tired too. Tietjens, who had been lying underneath the table, rose up and went into the least-exposed veranda as soon as her master moved to his own room, which was next to the stately chamber set apart for Tietjens. If a mere wife had wished to sleep out-of-doors in that pelting rain, it would not have mattered, but Tietjens was a dog, and therefore the better animal. I looked at Strickland, expecting to see him flog her with a whip. He smiled queerly, as a man would smile after telling some hideous domestic tragedy. "She has done this ever since I moved in here."

The dog was Strickland's dog, so I said nothing, but I felt all that Strickland felt in being made light of. Tietjens encamped outside my bedroom window, and storm after storm came up, thundered on the thatch, and died away. The lightning spattered the sky as a thrown egg spatters a barn door, but the light was pale blue, not yellow; and looking through my slit bamboo blinds, I could see the great dog standing, not sleeping, in the veranda, the hackles alift on her back, and her feet planted as tensely as the drawn wire rope of a suspension bridge. In the very short pauses of the thunder I tried to sleep, but it seemed that some one wanted me very badly. He, whoever he was, was trying to call me by name, but his voice was no more than a husky whisper. Then the thunder ceased and Tietjens went into the garden and howled at the low moon. Somebody tried to open my door, and walked about and through the house, and stood breathing heavily in the verandas, and just when I was falling asleep I fancied that I heard a wild hammering and clamoring above my head or on the door.

I ran into Strickland's room and asked him whether he was ill and had been calling for me. He was lying on the bed half-dressed, with a pipe in his mouth. "I thought you'd come," he said. "Have I been walking around the house at all?"

I explained that he had been in the dining-room and the smoking-room and two or three other places; and he laughed and told me to go back to bed. I went back to bed and slept till the morning, but in all my dreams I was sure I was doing some one an injustice in not attending to his wants. What those wants were I could not tell, but a fluttering, whispering, bolt-fumbling, luring, loitering some one was reproaching me for my slackness, and through all the dreams I heard the howling of Tietjens in the garden and the thrashing of the rain.

I was in that house for two days, and Strickland went to his office daily, leaving me alone for eight or ten hours a day, with Tietjens for my only companion. As long as the full light lasted I was comfortable, and so was Tietjens; but in the twilight she and I moved into the back veranda and cuddled each other for company. We were alone in the house, but for all that it was fully occupied by a tenant with whom I had no desire to interfere. I never saw him, but I could see the curtains between the rooms quivering where he had just passed through; I could hear the chairs creaking as the bamboos sprung under a weight that had just quitted them; and I could feel when I went to get a book from the dining-room that somebody was waiting in the shadows of the front veranda till I should have gone away. Tietjens made the twilight more interesting by glaring into the darkened rooms, with every hair erect, and following the motions of something that I could not see. She never entered the rooms, but her eyes moved, and that was quite sufficient. Only when my servant came to trim the lamps and made all light and habitable, she would come in with me and spend her time sitting on her haunches watching an invisible extra man as he moved about behind my shoulder. Dogs are cheerful companions.

I explained to Strickland, gently as might be, that I would go over to the club and find for myself quarters there. I admired his hospitality, was pleased with his guns and rods, but I did not much care for his house and its atmosphere. He heard me out to the end, and then smiled very wearily, but without contempt, for he is a man who understands things. "Stay on," he said, "and see what this thing means. All you have talked about I have known since I took the bungalow. Stay on and wait. Tietjens has left me. Are you going too?"

I had seen him through one little affair connected with an idol that had brought me to the doors of a lunatic asylum, and I had no desire to help him through further experiences. He was a man to whom unpleasantnesses arrived as do dinners to ordinary people.

Therefore I explained more clearly than ever that I liked him immensely, and would be happy to see him in the daytime, but that I didn't care to sleep under his roof. This was after dinner, when Tietjens had gone out to lie in the veranda.

" 'Pon my soul, I don't wonder," said Strickland, with his eyes on the ceiling-cloth. "Look at that!"

The tails of two snakes were hanging between the cloth and the cornice of the wall. They threw long shadows in the lamp-light. "If you are afraid of snakes, of course—" said Strickland. "I hate and fear snakes, because if you look into the eyes of any snake you will see that it knows all and more of man's fall, and that it feels all the contempt that the devil felt when Adam was exicted from Eden. Besides which its bite is generally fatal, and it bursts up trouser legs."

"You ought to get your thatch overhauled," I said. "Give me a masheer rod, and we'll poke 'em down."

"They'll hide among the roof beams," said Strickland. "I can't stand snakes overhead. I'm going up. If I shake 'em down, stand by with a cleaning-rod and break their backs."

I was not anxious to assist Strickland in his work, but I took the loading-rod and waited in the dining-room, while Strickland brought a gardener's ladder from the veranda and set it against the side of the room. The snake tails drew themselves up and disappeared. We could hear the dry rushing scuttle of long bodies running over the baggy cloth. Strickland took a lamp with him, while I tried to make clear the danger of hunting roof snakes between a ceiling-cloth, and a thatch, apart from the deterioration of property caused by ripping out ceiling-cloths.

"Nonsense!" said Strickland. "They're sure to hide near the walls by the cloth. The bricks are too cold for 'em, and the heat of the room is just what they like." He put his hand to the corner of the cloth and ripped the rotten stuff from the cornice. It gave a great sound of tearing, and Strickland put his head through the opening into the dark of the angle of the roof beams. I set my teeth and lifted the loading-rod, for I had not the least knowledge of what might descend.

"H'm," said Strickland; and his voice rolled and rumbled in the roof. "There's room for another set of rooms up here, and, by Jove! some one is occupying 'em."

"Snakes?" I said down below.

"No. It's a buffalo. Hand me up the two first joints of a masheer rod, and I'll prod it. It's lying on the main beam."

I handed up the rod.

"What a nest for owls and serpents. No wonder the snakes live here," said Strickland, climbing further into the roof. I could see his elbow thrusting with the rod. "Come out of that, whoever you are! Look out! Heads below there! It's tottering."

I saw the ceiling-cloth nearly in the center of the room bag with a shape that was pressing it downward and downward toward the lighted lamps on the table. I snatched a lamp out of danger and stood back. Then the cloth ripped out from the walls, tore, split, swayed, and shot down upon the table something that I dared not look at till Strickland had slid down the ladder and was standing by my side.

He did not say much, being a man of few words, but he picked up the loose end of the table-cloth and threw it over the thing on the table.

"It strikes me," said he, pulling down the

lamp, "our friend Imray has come back. Oh! you would, would you?"

There was a movement under the cloth, and a little snake wriggled out, to be back-broken by the butt of the masheer rod. I was sufficiently sick to make no remarks worth recording.

Strickland meditated and helped himself to drinks liberally. The thing under the cloth made no more signs of life.

"Is it Imray?" I said.

Strickland turned back the cloth for a moment and looked. "It is Imray," he said, "and his throat is cut from ear to ear."

Then we spoke both together and to ourselves: "That's why he whispered about the house."

Tietjens, in the garden, began to bay furiously. A little later her great nose heaved upon the dining-room door.

She sniffed and was still. The broken and tattered ceiling-cloth hung down almost to the level of the table, and there was hardly room to move away from the discovery.

Then Tietjens came in and sat down, her teeth bared and her forepaws planted. She looked at Strickland.

"It's bad business, old lady," said he. "Men don't go up into the roofs of their bungalows to die, and they don't fasten up the ceiling-cloth behind 'em. Let's think it out."

"Let's think it out somewhere else," I said.

"Excellent idea! Turn the lamps out. We'll get into my room."

I did not turn the lamps out. I went into Strickland's room first and allowed him to make the darkness. Then he followed me, and we lighted tobacco and thought. Strickland did the thinking. I smoked furiously because I was afraid.

"Imray is back," said Strickland. "The question is, who killed Imray? Don't talk—I have a notion of my own. When I took this bungalow I took most of Imray's servants. Imray was guileless and inoffensive, wasn't he?"

I agreed, though the heap under the cloth looked neither one thing nor the other.

"If I call the servants they will stand fast in a crowd and lie like Aryans. What do you suggest?"

"Call 'em in one by one," I said.

"They'll run away and give the news to all their fellows," said Strickland.

"We must segregate 'em. Do you suppose your servant knows anything about it?"

"He may, for aught I know, but I don't think it's likely. He has only been here two or three days."

"What's your notion?" I asked.

"I can't quite tell. How the dickens did the man get the wrong side of the ceiling-cloth?"

There was a heavy coughing outside Strickland's bedroom door. This showed that Bahadur

Khan, his body-servant, had waked from sleep and wished to put Strickland to bed.

"Come in," said Strickland. "It is a very warm night, isn't it?"

Bahadur Khan, a great, green-turbaned six-foot Mohammedan, said that it was a very warm night, but that there was more rain pending, which, by his honor's favor, would bring relief to the country.

"It will be so, if God pleases," said Strickland, tugging off his boots. "It is in my mind, Bahadur Khan, that I have worked thee remorselessly for many days—ever since that time when thou first camest into my service. What time was that?"

"Has the heaven-born forgotten? It was when Imray Sahib went secretly to Europe without warning given, and I—even I—came into the honored service of the protector of the poor."

"And Imray Sahib went to Europe?"

"It is so said among the servants."

"And thou wilt take service with him when he returns?"

"Assuredly, sahib. He was a good master and cherished his dependents."

"That is true. I am very tired, but I can go buck-shooting to-morrow. Give me the little rifle that I use for black buck; it is in the case yonder."

The man stooped over the case, handed barrels, stock, and fore-end to Strickland, who fitted them together. Yawning dolefully, then he reached

down to the gun-case, took a solid drawn cartridge, and slipped it into the breech of the .360
express.

"And Imray Sahib has gone to Europe
secretly? That is very strange, Bahadur Khan,
is it not?"

"What do I know of the ways of the white
man, heaven-born?"

"Very little, truly. But thou shalt know more.
It has reached me that Imray Sahib has returned
from his so long journeyings, and that even now
he lies in the next room, waiting his servant."

"Sahib!"

The lamp-light slid along the barrels of the
rifle as they leveled themselves against Bahadur
Khan's broad breast.

"Go, then, and look!" said Strickland. "Take
a lamp. Thy master is tired, and he waits. Go!"

The man picked up a lamp and went into the
dining-room, Strickland following, and almost
pushing him with the muzzle of the rifle. He
looked for a moment at the black depths behind
the ceiling-cloth, at the carcass of the mangled
snake under foot, and last, a gray glaze setting on
his face, at the thing under the table-cloth.

"Hast thou seen?" said Strickland, after a
pause.

"I have seen. I am clay in the white man's
hands. What does the presence do?"

"Hang thee within a month! What else?"

"For killing him? Nay, sahib, consider. Walking among us, his servants, he cast his eyes upon my child, who was four years old. Him he bewitched, and in ten days he died of the fever. My child!"

"What said Imray Sahib?"

"He said he was a handsome child, and patted him on the head; wherefore my child died. Wherefore I killed Imray Sahib in the twilight, when he came back from office and was sleeping. The heaven-born knows all things. I am the servant of the heaven-born."

Strickland looked at me above the rifle, and said, in the vernacular: "Thou art witness to this saying. He has killed."

Bahadur Khan stood ashen gray in the light of the one lamp. The need for justification came upon him very swiftly.

"I am trapped," he said, "but the offense was that man's. He cast an evil eye upon my child, and I killed and hid him. Only such as are served by devils," he glared at Tietjens, crouched stolidly before him, "only such could know what I did."

"It was clever. But thou shouldst have lashed him to the beam with a rope. Now, thou thyself wilt hang by a rope. Orderly!"

A drowsy policeman answered Strickland's call. He was followed by another, and Tietjens sat still.

"Take him to the station," said Strickland. "There is a case toward."

"Do I hang, then?" said Bahadur Khan, making no attempt to escape and keeping his eyes on the ground.

"If the sun shines, or the water runs, thou wilt hang," said Strickland. Bahadur Khan stepped back one pace, quivered, and stood still. The two policemen waited further orders.

"Go!" said Strickland.

"Nay; but I go very swiftly," said Bahadur Khan. "Look! I am even now a dead man."

He lifted his foot, and to the little toe there clung the head of the half-killed snake, firm fixed in the agony of death.

"I come of land-holding stock," said Bahadur Khan, rocking where he stood. "It were a disgrace for me to go to the public scaffold, therefore I take this way. Be it remembered that the sahib's shirts are correctly enumerated, and that there is an extra piece of soap in his wash-basin. My child was bewitched, and I slew the wizard. Why should you seek to slay me? My honor is saved, and—and—I die."

At the end of an hour he died as they die who are bitten by the little kariat, and the policemen bore him and the thing under the table-cloth to their appointed places. They were needed to make clear the disappearance of Imray.

"This," said Strickland, very calmly, as he climbed into bed, "is called the nineteenth century. Did you hear what that man said?"

"I heard," I answered. "Imray made a mistake."

"Simply and solely through not knowing the nature and coincidence of a little seasonal fever. Bahadur Khan had been with him for four years."

I shuddered. My own servants had been with me for exactly that length of time. When I went over to my own room I found him waiting, impassive as the copper head on a penny, to pull off my boots.

"What has befallen Bahadur Khan?" said I.

"He was bitten by a snake and died; the rest the sahib knows," was the answer.

"And how much of the matter hast thou known?"

"As much as might be gathered from one coming in the twilight to seek satisfaction. Gently, sahib. Let me pull off those boots."

I had just settled to the sleep of exhaustion when I heard Strickland shouting from his side of the house:

"Tietjens has come back to her room!"

And so she had. The great deerhound was couched on her own bedstead, on her own blanket, and in the next room the idle, empty ceiling-cloth wagged light-heartedly as it flailed on the table.

MY OWN TRUE GHOST STORY

MY OWN TRUE GHOST STORY

As I came through the Desert thus it was—
As I came through the Desert.
The City of Dreadful Night.

SOMEWHERE in the Other World, where there
are books and pictures and plays and shop-
windows to look at, and thousands of men who
spend their lives in building up all four, lives a
gentleman who writes real stories about the real
insides of people; and his name is Mr. Walter
Besant. But he will insist upon treating his
ghosts—he has published half a workshopful of
them—with levity. He makes his ghost-seers
talk familiarly, and, in some cases, flirt outrage-
ously, with the phantoms. You may treat anything, from a Viceroy to a Vernacular Paper,
with levity; but you must behave reverently
towards a ghost, and particularly an Indian one.

There are, in this land, ghosts who take the
form of fat, cold, pobby corpses, and hide in trees
near the roadside till a traveler passes. Then
they drop upon his neck and remain. There are
also terrible ghosts of women who have died in
child-bed. These wander along the pathways at
dusk, or hide in the crops near a village, and call
seductively. But to answer their call is death in

this world and the next. Their feet are turned backwards that all sober men may recognize them. There are ghosts of little children who have been thrown into wells. These haunt well-curbs and fringes of jungles, and wail under the stars, or catch women by the wrist and beg to be taken up and carried. These and the corpse-ghosts, however, are only vernacular articles and do not attack Sahibs. No native ghost has yet been authentically reported to have frightened an Englishman; but many English ghosts have scared the life out of both white and black.

Nearly every other Station owns a ghost. There are said to be two at Simla, not counting the woman who blows the bellows at Syree dâk-bungalow on the Old Road; Mussoorie has a house haunted of a very lively Thing; a White Lady is supposed to do night-watchman round a house in Lahore; Dalhousie says that one of her houses "repeats" on autumn evenings all the incidents of a horrible horse-and-precipice accident; Murree has a merry ghost, and, now that she has been swept by cholera, will have room for a sorrowful one; there are Officers Quarters, in Mian Mir whose doors open without reason, and whose furniture is guaranteed to creak, not with the heat of June but with the weight of Invisibles who come to lounge in the chairs; Peshawar possesses houses that none will willingly rent; and there is something—not fever—wrong with a big bungalow in Allahabad. The older Provinces

simply bristle with haunted houses, and march
phantom armies along their main thoroughfares.

Some of the dâk-bungalows on the Grand
Trunk Road have handy little cemeteries in their
compound—witnesses to the "changes and
chances of this mortal life" in the days when
men drove from Calcutta to the Northwest.
These bungalows are objectionable places to put
up in. They are generally very old, always dirty,
while the *khansamah* is as ancient as the bungalow. He either chatters senilely, or falls into the
long trances of age. In both moods he is useless.
If you get angry with him, he refers to some
Sahib dead and buried these thirty years, and
says that when he was in that Sahib's service not
a *khansamah* in the Province could touch him.
Then he jabbers and mows and trembles and fid-
gets among the dishes and you repent of your irritation.

In these dâk-bungalows, ghosts are most likely
to be found, and when found, they should be
made a note of. Not long ago it was my business
to live in dâk-bungalows. I never inhabited the
same house for three nights running, and grew
to be learned in the breed. I lived in Govern-
ment-built ones with red brick walls and rail ceil-
ings, an inventory of the furniture posted in every
room, and an excited snake at the threshold to
give welcome. I lived in "converted" ones—old
houses officiating as dâk-bungalows—where
nothing was in its proper place and there wasn't

even a fowl for dinner. I lived in second-hand palaces where the wind blew through open-work marble tracery just as uncomfortably as through a broken pane. I lived in dâk-bungalows where the last entry in the visitors' book was fifteen months old, and where they slashed off the curry-kid's head with a sword. It was my good luck to meet all sorts of men, from sober traveling missionaries and deserters flying from British Regiments, to drunken loafers who threw whisky bottles at all who passed; and my still greater good fortune just to escape a maternity case. Seeing that a fair proportion of the tragedy of our lives out here acted itself in dâk-bungalows, I wondered that I had met no ghosts. A ghost that would voluntarily hang about a dâk-bungalow would be mad of course; but so many men have died mad in dâk-bungalows that there must be a fair percentage of lunatic ghosts.

In due time I found my ghost, or ghosts rather, for there were two of them. Up till that hour I had sympathized with Mr. Besant's method of handling them, as shown in *"The Strange Case of Mr. Lucraft and other Stories."* I am now in the opposition.

We will call the bungalow Katmal dâk-bungalow. But that was the smallest part of the horror. A man with a sensitive hide has no right to sleep in dâk-bungalows. He should marry. Katmal dâk-bungalow was old and rotten and un-repaired. The floor was of worn brick, the walls were filthy, and the windows were nearly black with grime. It stood on a by-path largely used by native Sub-Deputy Assistants of all kinds, from Finance to Forest; but real Sahibs were rare. The *khansamah,* who was nearly bent double with old age, said so.

When I arrived, there was a fitful, undecided rain on the face of the land, accompanied by a restless wind, and every gust made a noise like the rattling of dry bones in the stiff toddy-palms outside. The *khansamah* completely lost his head on my arrival. He had served a Sahib once. Did I know that Sahib? He gave me the name of a well-known man who has been buried for more than a quarter of a century, and showed me an ancient daguerreotype of that man in his prehistoric youth. I had seen a steel engraving of him at the head of a double volume of Memoirs a month before, and I felt ancient beyond telling.

The day shut in and the *khansamah* went to get me food. He did not go through the pretense of calling it *"khana"*—man's victuals. He said *"ratub,"* and that means, among other things, "grub"—dog's rations. There was no insult in his choice of the term. He had forgotten the other word, I suppose.

While he was cutting up the dead bodies of animals, I settled myself down, after exploring the dâk-bungalow. There were three rooms, beside my own, which was a corner kennel, each giving into the other through dingy white doors

fastened with long iron bars. The bungalow was
a very solid one, but the partition-walls of the
rooms were almost jerry-built in their flimsiness.
Every step or bang of a trunk echoed from my
room down the other three, and every footfall
came back tremulously from the far walls. For
this reason I shut the door. There were no lamps
—only candles in long glass shades. An oil wick
was set in the bath-room.

For bleak, unadulterated misery that dâk-
bungalow was the worst of the many that I had
ever set foot in. There was no fireplace, and the
windows would not open; so a brazier of char-
coal would have been useless. The rain and the
wind splashed and gurgled and moaned round the
house, and the toddy-palms rattled and roared.
Half a dozen jackals went through the compound
singing, and a hyena stood afar off and mocked
them. A hyena would convince a Sadducee of
the Resurrection of the Dead—the worst sort of
Dead. Then came the *ratub*—a curious meal,
half native and half English in composition—
with the old *khansamah* babbling behind my chair
about dead and gone English people, and the
wind-blown candles playing shadow-bo-peep with
the bed and the mosquito-curtains.

It was just the sort of dinner and evening to
make a man think of every single one of his past
sins, and of all the others that he intended to commit if he lived.

Sleep, for several hundred reasons, was not

easy. The lamp in the bath-room threw the most absurd shadows into the room, and the wind was beginning to talk nonsense.

Just when the reasons were drowsy with blood-sucking I heard the regular—"Let-us-take-and-heave-him-over" grunt of doolie-bearers in the compound. First one doolie came in, then a second, and then a third. I heard the doolie dumped on the ground, and the shutter in front of my door shook. "That's some one trying to come in," I said. But no one spoke, and I persuaded myself that it was the gusty wind. The shutter of the room next to mine was attacked, flung back, and the inner door opened. "That's some Sub-Deputy Assistant," I said, "and he has brought his friends with him. Now we'll talk and spit and smoke for an hour."

But there were no voices and no footsteps. No one was putting his luggage into the next room. The door shut, and I thanked Providence that I was to be left in peace. But I was curious to know where the doolies had gone. I got out of bed and looked into the darkness. There was never a sign of a doolie. Just as I was getting into bed again, I heard, in the next room, the sound that no man in his senses can possibly mistake—the whir of a billiard ball down the length of the slates when the striker is stringing for break. No other sound is like it. A minute afterwards there was another whir, and I got into bed. I was not frightened—indeed I was not. I was very curious to know what had become of the doolies. I jumped into bed for that reason.

Next minute I heard the double click of a cannon and my hair sat up. It is a mistake to say that hair stands up. The skin of the head tightens and you can feel a faint, prickly bristling all over the scalp. That is the hair sitting up.

There was a whir and a click, and both sounds could only have been made by one thing—a billiard ball. I argued the matter out at great length with myself; and the more I argued the less probable it seemed that one bed, one table, and two chairs—all the furniture of the room next to mine—could so exactly duplicate the sounds of a game of billiards. After another cannon, a three-cushion one to judge by the whir, I argued no more. I had found my ghost and would have given worlds to have escaped from that dâk-bungalow. I listened, and with each listen the game grew clearer. There was a whir on whir and click on click. Sometimes there was a double click and a whir and another click. Beyond any sort of doubt, people were playing billiards in the next room. And the next room was not big enough to hold a billiard table!

Between the pauses of the wind I heard the game go forward—stroke after stroke. I tried to believe that I could not hear voices; but that attempt was a failure.

Do you know what fear is? Not ordinary fear of insult, injury or death. but abject, quivering dread of something that you cannot see—fear that dries the inside of the mouth and half of the throat—fear that makes you sweat on the palms of the hands, and gulp in order to keep the uvula at work? This is a fine Fear—a great cowardice, and must be felt to be appreciated. The very improbability of billiards in a dâk-bungalow proved the reality of the thing. No man—drunk or sober—could imagine a game at billiards, or invent the spitting crack of a "screw-cannon."

A severe course of dâk-bungalows has this disadvantage—it breeds infinite credulity. If a man said to a confirmed dâk-bungalow-haunter:—"There is a corpse in the next room, and there's a mad girl in the next one, and the woman and man on that camel have just eloped from a place sixty miles away," the hearer would not disbelieve because he would know that nothing is too wild, grotesque, or horrible to happen in a dâk-bungalow.

This credulity, unfortunately, extends to ghosts. A rational person fresh from his own house would have turned on his side and slept. I did not. So surely as I was given up as a bad carcass by the scores of things in the bed because the bulk of my blood was in my heart, so surely did I hear every stroke of a long game at billiards played in the echoing room behind the iron-barred door. My dominant fear was that the players might want a marker. It was an absurd fear; because creatures who could play in the dark would

be above such superfluities. I only know that that
was my terror; and it was real.

After a long long while, the game stopped, and
the door banged. I slept because I was dead
tired. Otherwise I should have preferred to have
kept awake. Not for everything in Asia would I
have dropped the door-bar and peered into the
dark of the next room.

When the morning came, I considered that I
had done well and wisely and inquired for the
means of departure.

"By the way, *khansamah*," I said, "what were
those three doolies doing in my compound in the
night?"

"There were no doolies," said the *khansamah*.

I went into the next room and the daylight
streamed through the open door. I was immensely brave. I would, at that hour, have
played Black Pool with the owner of the big
Black Pool down below.

"Has this place always been a dâk-bungalow?"
I asked.

"No," said the *khansamah*. "Ten or twenty
years ago, I have forgotten how long, it was a
billiard-room."

"A how much?"

"A billiard-room for the Sahibs who built the
Railway. I was *khansamah* then in the big
house where all the Railway-Sahibs lived, and I
used to come across with brandy-*shrab*. These
three rooms were all one, and they held a big table

on which the Sahibs played every evening. But the Sahibs are all dead now, and the Railway runs, you say, nearly to Kabul."

"Do you remember anything about the Sahibs?"

"It is long ago, but I remember that one Sahib, a fat man and always angry, was playing here one night, and he said to me:—'Mangal Khan, brandy *pani do*,' and I filled the glass, and he bent over the table to strike, and his head fell lower and lower till it hit the table, and his spectacles came off, and when we—the Sahibs and I myself —ran to lift him he was dead. I helped to carry him out. Aha, he was a strong Sahib! But he is dead and I, old Mangal Khan, am still living, by your favor."

That was more than enough! I had my ghost —a first-hand, authenticated article. I would write to the Society for Psychical Research—I would paralyze the Empire with the news! But I would, first of all, put eighty miles of assessed crop-land between myself and that dâk-bungalow before nightfall. The Society might send their regular agent to investigate later on.

I went into my own room and prepared to pack after noting down the facts of the case. As I smoked I heard the game begin again,—with a miss in balk this time, for the whir was a short one.

The door was open and I could see into the room. Click—click! That was a cannon. I entered the room without fear, for there was sunlight within and a fresh breeze without. The unseen game was going on at a tremendous rate. And well it might, when a restless little rat was running to and fro inside the dingy ceiling-cloth, and a piece of loose window-sash was making fifty breaks off the window-bolt as it shook in the breeze!

Impossible to mistake the sound of billiard balls! Impossible to mistake the whir of a ball over the slate! But I was to be excused. Even when I shut my enlightened eyes the sound was marvelously like that of a fast game.

Entered angrily the faithful partner of my sorrows, Kadir Baksh.

"This bungalow is very bad and low caste! No wonder the Presence was disturbed and is speckled. Three sets of doolie-bearers came to the bungalow late last night when I was sleeping outside, and said that it was their custom to rest in the rooms set apart for the English people! What honor has the *khansamah?* They tried to enter, but I told them to go. No wonder, if these *Oorias* have been here, that the Presence is sorely spotted. It is shame, and the work of a dirty man."

Kadir Baksh did not say that he had taken from each gang two annas for rent in advance, and then, beyond my earshot, had beaten them with the big green umbrella whose use I could never before divine. But Kadir Baksh had no notion of morality.

There was an interview with the *khansamah*, but as he promptly lost his head, wrath gave place to pity, and pity led to a long conversation, in the course of which he put the fat Engineer-Sahib's tragic death in three separate stations—two of them fifty miles away. The third shift was to Calcutta, and there the Sahib died while driving a dog-cart.

If I had encouraged him the *khansamah* would have wandered all through Bengal with his corpse.

I did not go away as soon as I intended. I stayed for the night, while the wind and the rat and the sash and the window-bolt played a ding-dong "hundred and fifty up." Then the wind ran out and the billiards stopped, and I felt that I had ruined my one genuine, hall-marked ghost story.

Had I only stopped at the proper time, I could have made anything out of it.

That was the bitterest thought of all!

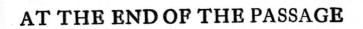

AT THE END OF THE PASSAGE

AT THE END OF THE PASSAGE

FOUR men, theoretically entitled to "life, liberty, and the pursuit of happiness," sat at a table playing whist. The thermometer marked—for them—one hundred and one degrees of heat. The room was darkened till it was only just possible to distinguish the pips of the cards and the very white faces of the players. A tattered, rotten punkah of whitewashed calico was puddling the hot air and whining dolefully at each stroke. Outside lay gloom of a November day in London. There was neither sky, sun, nor horizon—nothing but a brown-purple haze of heat. It was as though the earth were dying of apoplexy.

From time to time clouds of tawny dust rose from the ground without wind or warning, flung themselves table-clothwise among the tops of the parched trees, and came down again. Then a whirling dust-devil would scutter across the plain for a couple of miles, break and fall outward, though there was nothing to check its flight save a long low line of piled railway-sleepers white with the dust, a cluster of huts made of mud, condemned rails and canvas, and the one squat four-roomed bungalow that belonged to the assistant engineer in charge of a section of the Gandhari State line then under construction.

119

The four men, stripped to the thinnest of sleep-ing-suits, played whist crossly, with wranglings as to leads and returns. It was not the best kind of whist, but they had taken some trouble to ar-rive at it. Mottram, of the Indian Survey, had ridden thirty and railed one hundred miles from his lonely post in the desert since the previous night; Lowndes, of the Civil Service, on special duty in the political department, had come as far to escape for an instant the miserable intrigues of an impoverished native state whose king alter-nately fawned and blustered for more money from the pitiful revenues contributed by hard-wrung peasants and despairing camel-breeders; Spurstow, the doctor of the line, had left a cholera-stricken camp of coolies to look after itself for forty-eight hours while he associated with white men once more. Hummil, the assistant en-gineer, was the host. He stood fast, and received his friends thus every Sunday if they could come in. When one of them failed to appear, he would send a telegram to his last address, in order that he might know whether the defaulter was dead or alive. There be very many places in the East where it is not good or kind to let your acquaint-ances drop out of sight even for one short week.

The players were not conscious of any special regard for each other. They squabbled when-ever they met; but they ardently desired to meet, as men without water desire to drink. They were lonely folk who understood the dread meaning of loneliness. They were all under thirty years of age—which is too soon for any man to possess that knowledge.

"Pilsener," said Spurstow, after the second rubber, mopping his forehead.

"Beer's out, I'm sorry to say, and there's hardly enough soda-water for to-night," said Hummil.

"What filthy bad management!" snarled Spurstow.

"Can't help it. I've written and wired; but the trains don't come through regularly yet. Last week the ice ran out—as Lowndes knows."

"Glad I didn't come. I could ha' sent you some if I had known, though. Phew! it's too hot to go on playing bumblepuppy."

This was a savage growl at Lowndes, who only laughed. He was a hardened offender.

Mottram rose from the table and looked out of a chink in the shutters.

"What a sweet day!" said he.

The company yawned unanimously and betook themselves to an aimless investigation of all Hummil's possessions—guns, tattered novels, saddlery, spurs, and the like. They had fingered them a score of times before, but there was really nothing else to do.

"Got anything fresh?" said Lowndes.

"Last week's 'Gazette of India,' and a cutting from a home paper. My father sent it out. It's rather amusing."

"One of those vestrymen that call 'emselves

M. P.'s again, is it?" said Spurstow, who read his newspapers when he could get them.

"Yes. Listen to this. It's to your address, Lowndes. The man was making a speech to his constituents, and he piled it on. Here's a sample: 'And I assert unhesitatingly that the Civil Service in India is the preserve—the pet preserve—of the aristocracy of England. What does the democracy—what do the masses—get from that country, which we have step by step fraudulently annexed? I answer, nothing whatever. It is farmed, with a single eye to their own interests, by the scions of the aristocracy. They take good care to maintain their lavish scale of incomes, to avoid or stifle any inquiries into the nature and conduct of their administration, while they themselves force the unhappy peasant to pay with the sweat of his brow for all the luxuries in which they are lapped.'" Hummil waved the cutting above his head. "'Ear! 'ear!" said his audience.

Then Lowndes, meditatively: "I'd give—I'd give three months' pay to have that gentleman spend one month with me and see how the free and independent native prince works things. Old Timbersides"—this was his flippant title for an honored and decorated prince—"has been wearing my life out this week past for money. By Jove! his latest performance was to send me one of his women as a bribe!"

"Good for you. Did you accept it?" said Mottram.

"No. I rather wish I had, now. She was a pretty little person, and she yarned away to me about the horrible destitution among the king's women-folk. The darlings haven't had any new clothes for nearly a month, and the old man wants to buy a new drag from Calcutta—solid silver railings and silver lamps, and trifles of that kind. I've tried to make him understand that he has played the deuce with the revenues for the last twenty years, and must go slow. He can't see it."

"But he has the ancestral treasure-vault to draw on. There must be three millions at least in jewels and coin under his palace," said Hummil.

"Catch a native king disturbing the family treasure! The priests forbid it, except as the last resort. Old Timbersides has added something like a quarter of a million to the deposit in his reign."

"Where the mischief does it all come from?" said Mottram.

"The country. The state of the people is enough to make you sick. I've known the tax-men wait by a milch-camel till the foal was born, and then hurry off the mother for arrears. And what can I do? I can't get the court clerks to give me any accounts; I can't raise anything more than a fat smile from the commander-in-chief when I find out the troops are three months in arrears; and old Timbersides begins to weep when I speak to him. He has taken to the king's peg heavily—liquor brandy for whisky and Heidsieck for soda-water."

"That what's the Rao of Jubela took to. Even a native can't last long at that," said Spurstow. "He'll go out."

"And a good thing, too. Then I suppose we'll have a council of regency, and a tutor for the young prince, and hand him back his kingdom with ten years' accumulations."

"Whereupon that young prince, having been taught all the vices of the English, will play ducks and drakes with the money, and undo ten years' work in eighteen months. I've seen that business before," said Spurstow. "I should tackle the king with a light hand, if I were you, Lowndes. They'll hate you quite enough under any circumstances."

"That's all very well. The man who looks on can talk about the light hand; but you can't clean a pig-sty with a pen dipped in rosewater. I know my risks; but nothing has happened yet. My servant's an old Pathan, and he cooks for me. They are hardly likely to bribe him, and I don't accept food from my true friends, as they call themselves. Oh, but it's weary work! I'd sooner be with you, Spurstow. There's shooting near your camp."

"Would you? I don't think it. About fifteen deaths a day don't incite a man to shoot anything but himself. And the worst of it is that the poor devils look at you as though you ought to save them. Lord knows, I've tried everything. My last attempt was empirical, but it pulled an old man through. He was brought to me apparently past hope, and I gave him gin and Worcester sauce with cayenne. It cured him; but I don't recommend it."

"How do the cases run generally?" said Hummil.

"Very simply indeed. Chlorodyne, opium pill, collapse, nitre, bricks to the feet, and then—the burning-ghat. The last seems to be the only thing that stops the trouble. It's black cholera, you know. Poor devils! But, I will say, little Bunsee Lal, my apothecary, works like a demon. I've recommended him for promotion if he comes through it all alive."

"And what are your chances, old man?" said Mottram.

"Don't know; don't care much; but I've sent the letter in. What are you doing with yourself generally?"

"Sitting under a table in the tent and spitting on the sextant to keep it cool," said the man of the survey. "Washing my eyes to avoid ophthalmia, which I shall certainly get, and trying to make a sub-surveyor understand that an error of five degrees in an angle isn't quite so small as it looks. I'm altogether alone, y' know, and shall be till the end of the hot weather."

"Hummil's the lucky man," said Lowndes, flinging himself into a long chair. "He has an actual roof—torn as to the ceiling-cloth—but still a roof—over his head. He sees one train daily. He can get beer and soda-water, and ice it when God is good. He has books, pictures"—they were torn from the "Graphic"—"and the society of the excellent sub-contractor Jevins, besides the pleasure of receiving us weekly."

Hummil smiled grimly. "Yes, I'm the lucky man, I suppose. Jevins is luckier."

"How? Not—"

"Yes. Went out. Last Monday."

"*Ap se?*" said Spurstow, quickly, hinting the suspicion that was in everybody's mind. There was no cholera near Hummil's section. Even fever gives a man at least a week's grace, and sudden death generally implied self-slaughter.

"I judge no man this weather," said Hummil. "He had a touch of the sun, I fancy; for last week, after you fellows had left, he came into the veranda, and told me he was going home to see his wife, in Market Street, Liverpool, that evening. I got the apothecary in to look at him, and we tried to make him lie down. After an hour or two he rubbed his eyes and said he believed he had had a fit—hoped he hadn't said anything rude. Jevins had a great idea of better-ing himself socially. He was very like Chucks in his language."

"Well?"

"Then he went to his own bungalow and began cleaning a rifle. He told the servant that he was going after buck in the morning. Naturally he fumbled with the trigger, and shot himself through the head accidentally. The apothecary sent in a report to my chief, and Jevins is buried somewhere out there. I'd have wired to you, Spurstow, if you could have done anything."

"You're a queer chap," said Mottram. "If you killed the man yourself you couldn't have been more quiet about the business."

"Good Lord! what does it matter?" said Hummil, calmly. "I've got to do a lot of his overseeing work in addition to my own. I'm the only person that suffers. Jevins is out of it—by pure accident, of course, but out of it. The apothecary was going to write a long screed on suicide. Trust a babu to drivel when he gets the chance."

"Why didn't you let it go in as suicide?" said Lowndes.

"No direct proof. A man hasn't many privileges in this country, but he might at least be allowed to mishandle his own rifle. Besides, some day I may need a man to smother up an accident to myself. Live and let live. Die and let die."

"You take a pill," said Spurstow, who had been watching Hummil's white face narrowly. "Take a pill, and don't be an ass. That sort of talk is skittles. Anyhow, suicide is shirking your work. If I was a Job ten times over, I should be so interested in what was going to happen next that I'd stay on and watch."

"Ah! I've lost that curiosity," said Hummil.

"Liver out of order?" said Lowndes, feelingly.

"No. Can't sleep. That's worse."

"By Jove, it is!" said Mottram. "I'm that way every now and then, and the fit has to wear itself out. What do you take for it?"

"Nothing. What's the use? I haven't had ten minutes' sleep since Friday morning."

"Poor chap! Spurstow, you ought to attend to this," said Mottram. "Now you mention it, your eyes are rather gummy and swollen."

Spurstow, still watching Hummil, laughed lightly. "I'll patch him up later on. Is it too hot, do you think, to go for a ride?"

"Where to?" said Lowndes, wearily. "We shall have to go away at eight, and there'll be riding enough for us then. I hate a horse, when I have to use him as a necessity. Oh, heavens! what is there to do?"

"Begin whist again, at chick points" (a "chick" is supposed to be eight shillings), "and a gold mohur on the rub," said Spurstow, promptly.

"Poker. A month's pay all round for the pool —no limit—and fifty-rupee raises. Somebody would be broken before we got up," said Lowndes.

"Can't say that it would give me any pleasure to break any man in this company," said Mottram. "There isn't enough excitement in it, and it's foolish." He crossed over to the worn and battered little camp-piano—wreckage of a mar-

ried household that had once held the bungalow
—and opened the case.

"It's used up long ago," said Hummil. "The
servants have picked it to pieces."

The piano was indeed hopelessly out of order,
but Mottram managed to bring the rebellious
notes into a sort of agreement, and there rose
from the ragged key-board something that might
once have been the ghost of a popular music-
hall song. The men in the long chairs turned
with evident interest as Mottram banged the
more lustily.

"That's good!" said Lowndes. "By Jove! the
last time I heard that song was in '79, or there-
abouts, just before I came out."

"Ah!" said Spurstow, with pride, "I was home
in '80." And he mentioned a song of the streets
popular at that date.

Mottram executed it indifferently well.
Lowndes criticized, and volunteered emendations.
Mottram dashed into another ditty, not of the
music-hall character, and made as if to rise.

"Sit down," said Hummil. "I didn't know that
you had any music in your composition. Go on
playing until you can't think of anything more.
I'll have that piano tuned up before you come
again. Play something festive."

Very simple indeed were the tunes to which
Mottram's art and the limitations of the piano
could give effect, but the men listened with pleasure, and in the pauses talked all together of what

they had seen or heard when they were last at home. A dense dust-storm sprung up outside and swept roaring over the house, enveloping it in the choking darkness of midnight, but Mottram continued unheeding, and the crazy tinkle reached the ears of the listeners above the flapping of the tattered ceiling-cloth.

In the silence after the storm he glided from the more directly personal songs of Scotland, half humming them as he played, into the "Evening Hymn."

"Sunday," said he nodding his head.

"Go on. Don't apologize for it," said Spurstow.

Hummil laughed long and riotously. "Play it, by all means. You're full of surprises to-day. I didn't know you had such a gift of finished sarcasm. How does that thing go?"

Mottram took up the tune.

"Too slow by half. You miss the note of gratitude," said Hummil. "It ought to go to the 'Grasshopper Polka'—this way." And he chanted, *prestissimo*:

> "'Glory to Thee, my God, this night,
> For all the blessings of the light.'

That shows we really feel our blessings. How does it go on?—

> "'If in the night I sleepless lie,
> My soul with sacred thoughts supply,
> May no ill dreams disturb my rest,'—

Quicker, Mottram!—

"'Or powers of darkness me molest.'"

"Bah! what an old hypocrite you are."

"Don't be an ass," said Lowndes. "You are at full liberty to make fun of anything else you like, but leave that hymn alone. It's associated in my mind with the most scared recollections—"

"Summer evenings in the country—stained-glass window—light going out, and you and she jamming your heads together over one hymn-book," said Mottram.

"Yes, and a fat old cockchafer hitting you in the eye when you walked home. Smell of hay, and a moon as big as a bandbox sitting on the top of a haycock; bats—roses—milk and midges," said Lowndes.

"Also mothers. I can just recollect my mother singing me to sleep with that when I was a little chap," said Spurstow.

The darkness had fallen on the room. They could hear Hummil squirming in his chair.

"Consequently," said he, testily, "you sing it when you are seven fathoms deep in hell! It's an insult to the intelligence of the Deity to pretend we're anything but tortured rebels."

"Take two pills," said Spurstow: "that's tortured liver."

"The usually placid Hummil is in a vile bad temper. I'm sorry for the coolies to-morrow," said Lowndes, as the servants brought in the lights and prepared the table for dinner.

As they were settling into their places about the miserable goat-chops, the curried eggs, and the smoked tapioca pudding, Spurstow took occasion to whisper to Mottram: "Well done, David!"

"Look after Saul, then," was the reply.

"What are you two whispering about?" said Hummil, suspiciously.

"Only saying that you are a d——d poor host. This fowl can't be cut," returned Spurstow, with a sweet smile. "Call this a dinner?"

"I can't help it. You don't expect a banquet, do you?"

Throughout that meal Hummil contrived laboriously to insult directly and pointedly all his guests in succession, and at each insult Spurstow kicked the aggrieved person under the table, but he dared not exchange a glance of intelligence with either of them. Hummil's face was white and pinched, while his eyes were unnaturally large. No man dreamed for a moment of resenting his savage personalities, but as soon as the meal was over they made haste to get away.

"Don't go. You're just getting amusing, you fellows. I hope I haven't said anything that annoyed you. You're such touchy devils." Then, changing the note into one of almost abject entreaty: "I say, you surely aren't going?"

"Where I dines, I sleeps, in the language of the

blessed Jorrocks," said Spurstow. "I want to have a look at your coolies to-morrow, if you don't mind. You can give me a place to lie down in, I suppose?"

The others pleaded the urgency of their several employs next day, and, saddling up, departed together, Hummil begging them to come next Sunday. As they jogged off together, Lowndes unbosomed himself to Mottram: ". . . And I never felt so like kicking a man at his own table in my life. Said I cheated at whist, and reminded me I was in debt! Told you you were as good as a liar to your face! You aren't half indignant enough over it."

"Not I," said Mottram. "Poor devil! Did you ever know old Hummy behave like that before? Did you ever know him go within a hundred miles of it?"

"That's no excuse. Spurstow was hacking my shin all the time, so I kept a hand on myself. Else I should have—"

"No, you wouldn't. You'd have done as Hummy did about Jevins: judge no man this weather. By Jove! the buckle of my bridle is hot in my hand! Trot out a bit, and mind the rat-holes."

Ten minutes' trotting jerked out of Lowndes one very sage remark when he pulled up, sweating from every pore:

"Good thing Spurstow's with him to-night."

"Ye-es. Good man, Spurstow. Our roads

turn here. See you again next Sunday, if the sun doesn't bowl me over."

"S'pose so, unless old Timbersides' finance minister manages to dress some of my food. Good-night, and—God bless you!"

"What's wrong now?"

"Oh, nothing." Lowndes gathered up his whip, and, as he flicked Mottram's mare on the flank, added: "You're a good little chap—that's all." And the mare bolted half a mile across the sand on the word.

In the assistant engineer's bungalow Spurstow and Hummil smoked the pipe of silence together, each narrowly watching the other. The capacity of a bachelor's establishment is as elastic as its arrangements are simple. A servant cleared away the dining-room table, brought in a couple of rude native bedsteads made of tape strung on a light wood frame, flung a square of cool Calcutta matting over each, set them side by side, pinned two towels to the punkah so that their fringes should just sweep clear of each sleeper's nose and mouth, and announced that the couches were ready.

The men flung themselves down, adjuring the punkah-coolies by all the powers of Eblis to pull. Every door and window was shut, for the outside air was that of an oven. The atmosphere within was only 104°, as the thermometer attested, and heavy with the foul smell of badly trimmed kerosene lamps; and this stench, combined with that of native tobacco, baked brick, and dried earth, sends the heart of many a strong man down to his boots, for it is the smell of the great Indian Empire when she turns herself for six months into a house of torment. Spurstow packed his pillows craftily, so that he reclined rather than lay, his head at a safe elevation above his feet. It is not good to sleep on a low pillow in the hot weather if you happen to be of thick-necked build, for you may pass with lively snores and gurglings from natural sleep into the deep slumber of heat-apoplexy.

"Pack your pillows," said the doctor, sharply, as he saw Hummil preparing to lie down at full-length.

The night-light was trimmed; the shadow of the punkah wavered across the room, and the flick of the punkah-towel and the soft whine of the rope through the wall-hole followed it. Then the punkah flagged, almost ceased. The sweat poured from Spurstow's brow. Should he go out and harangue the coolie? It started forward again with a savage jerk, and a pin came out of the towels. When this was replaced a tom-tom in the coolie lines began to beat with the steady throb of a swollen artery inside some brain-fevered skull. Spurstow turned on his side and swore gently. There was no movement on Hummil's part. The man had composed himself as rigidly as a corpse, his hands clinched at his sides. The respiration was too hurried for any suspicion of sleep. Spurstow looked at the set face. The jaws were clinched, and there was a pucker round the quivering eyelids.

"He's holding himself as tightly as ever he can," thought Spurstow. "What a sham it is! and what in the world is the matter with him?— Hummil!"

"Yes."

"Can't you get to sleep?"

"No."

"Head hot? Throat feeling bulgy? or how?"

"Neither, thanks. I don't sleep much, you know."

"Feel pretty bad?"

"Pretty bad, thanks. There is a tom-tom outside, isn't there? I thought it was my head at first. Oh, Spurstow, for pity's sake, give me something that will put me asleep—sound asleep —if it's only for six hours!" He sprung up. "I haven't been able to sleep naturally for days, and I can't stand it!—I can't stand it!"

"Poor old chap!"

"That's no use. Give me something to make me sleep. I tell you I'm nearly mad. I don't know what I say half my time. For three weeks I've had to think and spell out every word that has come through my lips before I dared say it. I had to get my sentences out down to the last word, for fear of talking drivel if I didn't. Isn't that enough to drive a man mad? I can't see things correctly now, and I've lost my sense of touch. Make me sleep. Oh, Spurstow, for the love of God, make me sleep sound. It isn't enough merely to let me dream. Let me sleep!"

"All right, old man, all right. Go slow. You aren't half as bad as you think." The flood-gates of reserve once broken, Hummil was clinging to him like a frightened child.

"You're pinching my arm to pieces."

"I'll break your neck if you don't do something for me. No, I didn't mean that. Don't be angry, old fellow." He wiped the sweat off himself as he fought to regain composure. "As a matter of fact, I'm a bit restless and off my oats, and perhaps you could recommend some sort of sleeping-mixture—bromide of potassium."

"Bromide of skittles! Why didn't you tell me this before? Let go of my arm, and I'll see if there's anything in my cigarette-case to suit your complaint." He hunted among his day-clothes, turned up the lamp, opened a little silver cigarette-case, and advanced on the expectant Hummil with the daintiest of fairy squirts.

"The last appeal of civilization," said he, "and a thing I hate to use. Hold out your arm. Well, your sleeplessness hasn't ruined your muscle; and what a thick hide it is! Might as well inject a buffalo subcutaneously. Now in a few minutes the morphia will begin working. Lie down and wait."

A smile of unalloyed and idiotic delight began to creep over Hummil's face. "I think," he whispered—"I think I'm going off now. Gad! it's positively heavenly! Spurstow, you must give me that case to keep; you—" The voice ceased as the head fell back.

"Not for a good deal," said Spurstow to the unconscious form. "And now, my friend, sleeplessness of your kind being very apt to relax the moral fiber in little matters of life and death, I'll just take the liberty of spiking your guns."

He padded into Hummil's saddle-room in his bare feet, and uncased a twelve-bore, an express, and a revolver. Of the first he unscrewed the nipples and hid them in the bottom of a saddlery-case; of the second he abstracted the lever, placing it behind a big wardrobe. The third he merely opened, and knocked the doll-head bolt of the grip up with the heel of a riding-boot.

"That settled," he said, as he shook the sweat off his hands. "These little precautions will at least give you time to turn. You have too much sympathy with gun-room accidents."

And as he rose from his knees, the thick muffled voice of Hummil cried in the doorway: "You fool!"

Such tones they use who speak in the lucid intervals of delirium to their friends a little before they die.

Spurstow jumped with sheer fright. Hummil stood in the doorway, rocking with helpless laughter.

"That was awf'ly good of you, I'm sure," he

said, very slowly, feeling for his words. "I don't intend to go out by my own hand at present. I say, Spurstow, that stuff won't work. What shall I do? What shall I do?" And panic terror stood in his eyes.

"Lie down and give it a chance. Lie down at once."

"I daren't. It will only take me half-way again, and I sha'n't be able to get away this time. Do you know it was all I could do to come out just now? Generally I am as quick as lightning; but you have clogged my feet. I was nearly caught."

"Oh, yes, I understand. Go and lie down."

"No, it isn't delirium; but it was an awfully mean trick to play on me. Do you know I might have died?"

As a sponge rubs a slate clean, so some power unknown to Spurstow had wiped out of Hummil's face all that stamped it for the face of a man, and he stood at the doorway in the expression of his lost innocence. He had slept back into terrified childhood.

"Is he going to die on the spot?" thought Spurstow. Then, aloud: "All right, my son. Come back to bed, and tell me all about it. You couldn't sleep; but what was all the rest of the nonsense?"

"A place—a place down there," said Hummil, with simple sincerity. The drug was acting on him by waves, and he was flung from the fear of a strong man to the fright of a child as his nerves gathered sense or were dulled.

"Good God! I've been afraid of it for months past, Spurstow. It has made every night hell to me; and yet I'm not conscious of having done anything wrong."

"Be still, and I'll give you another dose. We'll stop your nightmares, you unutterable idiot!"

"Yes, but you must give me so much that I can't get away. You must make me quite sleepy —not just a little sleepy. It's so hard to run then."

"I know it; I know it. I've felt it myself. The symptoms are exactly as you describe."

"Oh, don't laugh at me, confound you! Before this awful sleeplessness came to me, I've tried to rest on my elbow and put a spur in the bed to sting me when I fell back. Look!"

"By Jove! the man has been roweled like a horse! Ridden by the nightmare with a vengeance! And we all thought him sensible enough. Heaven send us understanding! You like to talk, don't you, old man?"

"Yes, sometimes. Not when I'm frightened. Then I want to run. Don't you?"

"Always. Before I give you your second dose, try to tell me exactly what your trouble is."

Hummil spoke in broken whispers for nearly ten minutes, while Spurstow looked into the pupils of his eyes and passed his hand before them once or twice.

At the end of the narrative the silver cigarette-case was produced, and the last words that Hum-

mil said as he fell back for the second time were:
"Put me quite to sleep; for if I'm caught, I die—
I die!"

"Yes, yes; we all do that sooner or later, thank
Heaven! who has set a term to our miseries," said
Spurstow, settling the cushions under the head.
"It occurs to me that unless I drink something, I
shall go out before my time. I've stopped sweating, and I wear a seventeen-inch collar." And he
brewed himself scalding hot tea, which is an excellent remedy against heat-apoplexy if you take
three or four cups of it in time. Then he watched
the sleeper.

"A blind face that cries and can't wipe its eyes.
H'm! Decidedly, Hummil ought to go on leave
as soon as possible; and, sane or otherwise, he
undoubtedly did rowel himself most cruelly.
Well, Heaven send us understanding!"

At midday Hummil rose, with an evil taste in
his mouth, but an unclouded eye and a joyful
heart.

"I was pretty bad last night, wasn't I?" said
he.

"I have seen healthier men. You must have
had a touch of the sun. Look here: if I write
you a swingeing medical certificate, will you apply
for leave on the spot?"

"No."

"Why not? You want it."

"Yes, but I can hold on till the weather's a little
cooler."

"Why should you, if you can get relieved on the spot?"

"Burkett is the only man who could be sent; and he's a born fool."

"Oh, never mind about the line. You aren't so important as all that. Wire for leave, if necessary."

Hummil looked very uncomfortable.

"I can hold on till the rains," he said, evasively.

"You can't. Wire to head-quarters for Burkett."

"I won't. If you want to know why, particularly, Burkett is married, and his wife's just had a kid, and she's up at Simla, in the cool, and Burkett has a very nice billet that takes him into Simla from Saturday to Monday. That little woman isn't at all well. If Burkett was transferred she'd try to follow him. If she left the baby behind she'd fret herself to death. If she came—and Burkett's one of those selfish little beasts who are always talking about a wife's place being with her husband—she'd die. It's murder to bring a woman here just now. Burkett has got the physique of a rat. If he came here he'd go out; and I know she hasn't any money, and I am pretty sure she'd go out too. I'm salted in a sort of way, and I'm not married. Wait till the rains, and then Burkett can get thin down here. It'll do him heaps of good."

"Do you mean to say that you intend to face

—what you have faced, for the next fifty-six nights?"

"Oh, it won't be so bad, now you've shown me a way out of it. I can always wire to you. Besides, now I've once got into the way of sleeping, it'll be all right. Anyhow, I shan't put in for leave. That's the long and the short of it."

"My great Scott! I thought all that sort of thing was dead and done with."

"Bosh! You'd do the same yourself. I feel a new man, thanks to that cigarette-case. You're going over to camp now, aren't you?"

"Yes; but I'll try to look you up every other day, if I can."

"I'm not bad enough for that. I don't want you to bother. Give the coolies gin and ketchup."

"Then you feel all right?"

"Fit to fight for my life, but not to stand out in the sun talking to you. Go along, old man, and bless you!"

Hummil turned on his heel to face the echoing desolation of his bungalow, and the first thing he saw standing in the veranda was the figure of himself. He had met a similar apparition once before, when he was suffering from overwork and the strain of the hot weather.

"This is bad—already," he said, rubbing his eyes. "If the thing slides away from me all in one piece, like a ghost, I shall know it is only my eyes and stomach that are out of order. If it walks, I shall know that my head is going."

He walked to the figure, which naturally kept at an unvarying distance from him, as is the use of all specters that are born of overwork. It slid through the house and dissolved into swimming specks within the eyeball as soon as it reached the burning light of the garden. Hummil went about his business till even. When he came into dinner he found himself sitting at the table. The thing rose and walked out hastily.

No living man knows what that week held for Hummil. An increase of the epidemic kept Spurstow in camp among the coolies, and all he could do was to telegraph to Mottram, bidding him go to the bungalow and sleep there. But Mottram was forty miles away from the nearest telegraph, and knew nothing of anything save the needs of the survey till he met early on Sunday morning Lowndes and Spurstow heading toward Hummil's for the weekly gathering.

"Hope the poor chap's in a better temper," said the former, swinging himself off his horse at the door. "I suppose he isn't up yet."

"I'll just have a look at him," said the doctor. "If he's asleep there's no need to wake him."

And an instant later, by the tone of Spurstow's voice calling upon them to enter, the men knew what had happened.

The punkah was still being pulled over the bed, but Hummil had departed this life at least three hours before.

The body lay on its back, hands clinched by

the side, as Spurstow had seen it lying seven nights previously. In the staring eyes were written terror beyond the expression of any pen.

Mottram, who had entered behind Lowndes, bent over the dead and touched the forehead lightly with his lips. "Oh, you lucky, lucky devil!" he whispered.

But Lowndes had seen the eyes, and had withdrawn shuddering to the other side of the room.

"Poor chap! poor chap! And the last time I met him I was angry. Spurstow, we should have watched him. Has he—"

Deftly Spurstow continued his investigation, ending by a search round the room.

"No, he hasn't," he snapped. "There's no trace of anything. Call in the servants."

They came, eight or ten or them, whispering and peering over each other's shoulders.

"When did you sahib go to bed?" said Spurstow.

"At eleven or ten, we think," said Hummil's personal servant.

"He was well then? But how should you know?"

"He was not ill, as far as our comprehension extended. But he had slept very little for three nights. This I know, because I saw him walking much, and especially in the heart of the night.

As Spurstow was arranging the sheet, a big, straight-necked hunting-spur tumbled on the ground. The doctor groaned. The personal servant peeped at the body.

"What do you think, Chuma?" said Spurstow, catching the look in the dark face.

"Heaven-born, in my poor opinion, this that was my master has descended into the Dark Places, and there has been caught, because he was not able to escape with sufficient speed. We have the spur for evidence that he fought with Fear. Thus have I seen men of my race do with thorns when a spell was laid upon them to overtake them in their sleeping hours and they dared not sleep."

"Chuma, you're a mud-head. Go out and prepare seals to be set on the sahib's property."

"God has made the heaven-born. God has made me. Who are we, to inquire into the dispensations of God? I will bid the other servants hold aloof while you are reckoning the tale of the sahib's property. They are all thieves, and would steal."

"As far as I can make out, he died from—oh, anything: stopping of the heart's action, heat-apoplexy, or some other visitation," said Spurstow to his companions. "We must make an inventory of his effects, and so on."

"He was scared to death," insisted Lowndes. "Look at those eyes! For pity's sake, don't let him be buried with them open!"

"Whatever it was, he's out of all the trouble now," said Mottram, softly.

Spurstow was peering into the open eyes.

"Come here," said he. "Can you see anything there?"

"I can't face it!" whimpered Lowndes. "Cover up the face! Is there any fear on earth that can turn a man into that likeness? It's ghastly. Oh, Spurstow, cover him up!"

"No fear—on earth," said Spurstow. Mottram leaned over his shoulder and looked intently.

"I see nothing except some gray blurs in the pupil. There can be nothing there, you know."

"Even so. Well, let's think. It'll take half a day to knock up any sort of coffin; and he must have died at midnight. Lowndes, old man, go out and tell the coolies to break ground next to Jevins' grave. Mottram, go round the house with Chuma and see that the seals are put on things. Send a couple of men to me here, and I'll arrange."

The strong-armed servants when they returned to their own kind told a strange story of the doctor sahib vainly trying to call their master back to life by magic arts—to wit, the holding of a little green box opposite each of the dead man's eyes, of a frequent clicking of the same, and of a bewildered muttering on the part of the doctor sahib, who subsequently took the little green box away with him.

The resonant hammering of a coffin-lid is no pleasant thing to hear, but those who have experience maintain that much more terrible is the soft swish of the bed-linen, the reeving and unreeving of the bed-tapes, when he who has fallen by the road-side is appareled for burial, sinking gradually as the tapes are tied over, till the swaddled shape touches the floor and there is no protest against the indignity of hasty disposal.

At the last moment Lowndes was seized with scruples of conscience. "Ought you to read the service—from beginning to end?" said he.

"I intend to. You're my senior as a civilian. You can take it, if you like."

"I didn't mean that for a moment. I only thought if we could get a chaplain from some-where—I'm willing to ride anywhere—and give poor Hummil a better chance. That's all."

"Bosh!" said Spurstow, as he framed his lips to the tremendous words that stand at the head of the burial service.

After breakfast they smoked a pipe in silence to the memory of the dead. Then said Spurstow, absently:

" 'Tisn't in medical science."

"What?"

"Things in a dead man's eyes."

"For goodness' sake, leave that horror alone!" said Lowndes. "I've seen a native die of fright when a tiger chivied him. I know what killed Hummil."

"The deuce you do! I'm going to try to see." And the doctor retreated into the bathroom with a Kodak camera, splashing and grunting for ten minutes. Then there was the sound of something being hammered to pieces, and Spurstow emerged, very white indeed.

"Have you got a picture?" said Mottram. "What does the thing look like?"

"Nothing there. It was impossible, of course. You needn't look, Mottram. I've torn up the films. There was nothing there. It was impossible."

"That," said Lowndes, very distinctly, watching the shaking hand striving to relight the pipe, "is a damned lie."

There was no further speech for a long time. The hot wind whistled without, and the dry trees sobbed. Presently the daily train, winking brass, burnished steel, and spouting steam, pulled up, panting in the intense glare. "We'd better go on that," said Spurstow. "Go back to work. I've written my certificate. We can't do any more good here. Come on."

No one moved. It is not pleasant to face railway journeys at midday in June. Spurstow gathered up his hat and whip, and, turning in the doorway, said:

> "There may be heaven—there must be hell,
>   Meantime, there is our life here. We-ell?"

But neither Mottram nor Lowndes had any answer to the question.

THE MAN WHO WOULD
BE KING

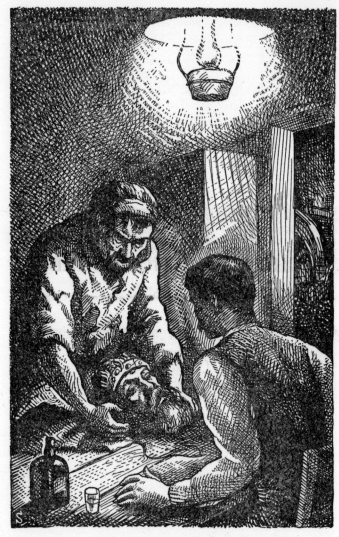

"The head of Daniel Dravot."

—*The Man Who Would Be King, p. 206*

THE MAN WHO WOULD BE KING

"Brother to a Prince and fellow to a beggar if he be found worthy."

THE Law, as quoted, lays down a fair conduct of life, and one not easy to follow. I have been fellow to a beggar again and again under circumstances which prevented either of us finding out whether the other was worthy. I have still to be brother to a Prince, though I once came near to kinship with what might have been a veritable King and was promised the reversion of a Kingdom—army, law-courts, revenue and policy all complete. But, to-day, I greatly fear that my King is dead, and if I want a crown I must go and hunt it for myself.

The beginning of everything was in a railway train upon the road to Mhow from Ajmir. There had been a Deficit in the Budget, which necessitated traveling, not Second-class, which is only half as dear as First-class, but by Intermediate, which is very awful indeed. There are no cushions in the Intermediate class, and the population are either Intermediate, which is Eurasian, or native, which for a long night journey is nasty, or Loafer, which is amusing though intoxicated. Intermediates do not patronize refreshment-rooms. They carry their food in bundles and pots, and buy sweets from the native sweetmeat-sellers, and drink the roadside water. That is why in the hot weather Intermediates are taken out of the carriages dead, and in all weathers are most properly looked down upon.

My particular Intermediate happened to be empty till I reached Nasirabad, when a huge gentleman in shirt-sleeves entered and following the custom of Intermediates, passed the time of day. He was a wanderer and a vagabond like myself, but with an educated taste for whisky. He told tales of things he had seen and done, of out-of-the-way corners of the Empire into which he had penetrated, and of adventures in which he risked his life for a few days' food. "If India was filled with men like you and me, not knowing more than the crows where they'd get their next day's rations, it isn't seventy millions of revenue the land would be paying—it's seven hundred millions," said he; and as I looked at his mouth and chin I was disposed to agree with him. We talked politics—the politics of Loaferdom that sees things from the underside where the lath and plaster is not smoothed off—and we talked postal arrangements because my friend wanted to send a telegram back from the next station to Ajmir, which is the turning-off place from the Bombay to the Mhow line as you travel westward. My friend had no money beyond eight annas which he wanted for dinner, and I had no money at all, owing to the hitch in the Budget before mentioned. Further, I was going into a wilderness where, though I should resume touch with the Treasury, there were no telegraph offices. I was, therefore, unable to help him in any way.

"We might threaten a Station-master, and make him send a wire on tick," said my friend, "but that'd mean inquiries for you and for me, and I've got my hands full these days. Did you say you are traveling back along this line within any days?"

"Within ten," I said.

"Can't you make it eight?" said he. "Mine is rather urgent business."

"I can send your telegram within ten days if that will serve you," I said.

"I couldn't trust the wire to fetch him now I think of it. It's this way. He leaves Delhi on the 23d for Bombay. That means he'll be running through Ajmir about the night of the 23d."

"But I'm going into the Indian Desert," I explained.

"Well and good," said he. "You'll be changing at Marwar Junction to get into Jodhpore territory—you must do that and he'll be coming through Marwar junction in the early morning of the 24th by the Bombay Mail. Can you be at Marwar Junction on that time? 'Twon't be inconveniencing you because I know that there's precious few pickings to be got out of these Central India States—even though you pretend to be correspondent of the *Backwoodsman*."

"Have you ever tried that trick?" I asked.

"Again and again, but the Residents find you out, and then you get escorted to the Border before you've time to get your knife into them. But about my friend here. I must give him a word o' mouth to tell him what's come to me or else he won't know where to go. I would take it more than kind of you if you was to come out of Central India in time to catch him at Marwar Junction, and say to him:—'He has gone South for the week.' He'll know what that means. He's a big man with a red beard, and a great swell he is. You'll find him sleeping like a gentleman with all his luggage round him in a Second-class compartment. But don't you be afraid. Slip down the window, and say:—'He has gone South for the week,' and he'll tumble. It's only cutting your time of stay in those parts by two days. I ask you as a stranger—going to the West," he said with emphasis.

"Where have you come from?" said I.

"From the East," said he, "and I am hoping that you will give him the message on the Square —for the sake of my Mother as well as your own."

Englishmen are not usually softened by appeals to the memory of their mothers, but for certain reasons, which will be fully apparent, I saw fit to agree.

"It's more than a little matter," said he, "and that's why I ask you to do it—and now I know

that I can depend on you doing it. A Second-
class carriage at Marwar Junction, and a red-
haired man asleep in it. You'll be sure to remember. I get out at the next station, and I must hold
on there till he comes or sends me what I want."

"I'll give the message if I catch him," I said,
"and for the sake of your Mother as well as mine
I'll give you a word of advice. Don't try to run
the Central India States just now as the correspondent of the *Backwoodsman*. There's a real
one knocking about here, and it might lead to
trouble."

"Thank you," said he simply, "and when will
the swine be gone? I can't starve because he's
ruining my work. I wanted to get hold of the
Degumber Rajah down here about his father's
widow, and give him a jump."

"What did he do to his father's widow, then?"

"Filled her up with red pepper and slippered
her to death as she hung from a beam. I found
that out myself and I'm the only man that would
dare going into the State to get hush-money for
it. They'll try to poison me, same as they did in
Chortumna when I went on the loot there. But
you'll give the man at Marwar Junction my message?"

He got out at a little roadside station, and I reflected. I had heard, more than once, of men per-
sonating correspondents of newspapers and bleeding small Native States with threats of exposure,
but I had never met any of the caste before.

They lead a hard life, and generally die with great suddenness. The Native States have a wholesome horror of English newspapers, which may throw light on their peculiar methods of government, and do their best to choke correspondents with champagne, or drive them out of their mind with four-in-hand barouches. They do not understand that nobody cares a straw for the internal administration of Native States so long as oppression and crime are kept within decent limits, and the ruler is not drugged, drunk, or diseased from one end of the year to the other. Native States were created by Providence in order to supply picturesque scenery, tigers, and tall-writing. They are the dark places of the earth, full of unimaginable cruelty, touching the Railway and the Telegraph on one side, and, on the other, the days of Harun-al-Raschid. When I left the train I did business with divers Kings, and in eight days passed through many changes of life. Sometimes I wore dress-clothes and consorted with Princes and Politicals, drinking from crystal and eating from silver. Sometimes I lay out upon the ground and devoured what I could get, from a plate made of a flapjack, and drank the running water, and slept under the same rug as my servant. It was all in the day's work.

Then I headed for the Great Indian Desert upon the proper date, as I had promised, and the night Mail set me down at Marwar Junction, where a funny little, happy-go-lucky, native-man-

aged railway runs to Jodhpore. The Bombay
Mail from Delhi makes a short halt at Marwar.
She arrived as I got in, and I had just time to
hurry to her platform and go down the carriages.
There was only one Second-class on the train. I
slipped into the window and looked down upon
a flaming red beard, half covered by a railway
rug. That was my man, fast asleep, and I dug
him gently in the ribs. He awoke with a grunt
and I saw his face in the light of the lamps. It
was a great and shining face.

"Tickets again?" said he.

"No," said I. "I am to tell you that he is gone
South for the week. He is gone South for the
week!"

The train had begun to move out. The red
man rubbed his eyes. "He has gone South for
the week," he repeated. "Now that's just like his
impudence. Did he say that I was to give you
anything?—'Cause I won't."

"He didn't," I said and dropped away, and
watched the red lights die out in the dark. It was
horribly cold because the wind was blowing off
the sands. I climbed into my own train—not an
Intermediate Carriage this time—and went to
sleep.

If the man with the beard had given me a rupee
I should have kept it as a memento of a rather
curious affair. But the consciousness of having
done my duty was my only reward.

Later on I reflected that two gentleman like

my friends could not do any good if they foregathered and personated correspondents of newspapers, and might, if they "stuck up" one of the
little rat-trap states of Central India or Southern
Rajputana get themselves into serious difficulties.
I therefore took some trouble to describe them as
accurately as I could remember to people who
would be interested in deporting them; and succeeded, so I was later informed, in having them
headed back from the Degumber borders.

Then I became respectable, and returned to an
Office where there were no Kings and no incidents except the daily manufacture of a newspaper. A newspaper office seems to attract every
conceivable sort of person, to the prejudice of discipline. Zenana-mission ladies arrive, and beg
that the Editor will instantly abandon all his
duties to describe a Christian prize-giving in a
back-slum of a perfectly inaccessible village;
Colonels who have been overpassed for commands
sit down and sketch the outline of a series of ten,
twelve, or twenty-four leading articles on Sen-
iority versus Selection; missionaries wish to know
why they have not been permitted to escape from
their regular vehicles of abuse and swear at a
brother-missionary under special patronage of
the editorial We; stranded theatrical companies
troop up to explain that they cannot pay for their
advertisements, but on their return from New
Zealand or Tahiti will do so with interest; in-
ventors of patent punkah-pulling machines, car-

riage couplings and unbreakable swords and axle-trees call with specifications in their pockets and hours at their disposal; tea-companies enter and elaborate their prospectuses with the office pens; secretaries of ball-committees clamor to have the glories of their last dance more fully expounded; strange ladies rustle in and say:—"I want a hundred lady's cards printed at once, please," which is manifestly part of an Editor's duty; and every dissolute ruffian that ever tramped the Grand Trunk Road makes it his business to ask for employment as a proof-reader. And, all the time, the telephone-bell is ringing madly, and Kings are being killed on the Continent, and Empires are saying—"You're another," and Mister Gladstone is calling down brimstone upon the British Dominions, and the little black copy-boys are whining, *"kaa-pi chay-ha-yeh"* (copy wanted) like tired bees, and most of the paper is as blank as Modred's shield.

But that is the amusing part of the year. There are other six months wherein none ever come to call, and the thermometer walks inch by inch up to the top of the glass, and the office is darkened to just about reading-light, and the press machines are red-hot of touch, and nobody writes anything but accounts of amusements in the Hill-stations, or obituary notices. Then the telephone becomes a tinkling terror, because it tells you of the sudden deaths of men and women that you knew intimately, and the prickly-heat covers you as with a garment, and you sit down and write:—"A slight increase of sickness is reported from the Khuda Janta Khan District. The outbreak is purely sporadic in its nature, and, thanks to the energetic efforts of the District authorities, is now almost at an end. It is, however, with deep regret we record the death, etc."

Then the sickness really breaks out, and the less recording and reporting the better for the peace of the subscribers. But the Empires and the Kings continue to divert themselves as selfishly as before, and the Foreman thinks that a daily paper really ought to come out once in twenty-four hours, and all the people at the Hill-stations in the middle of their amusements say: "Good gracious! Why can't the paper be sparkling? I'm sure there's plenty going on up here."

That is the dark half of the moon, and, as the advertisements say, "must be experienced to be appreciated."

It was in that season, and a remarkably evil season, that the paper began running the last issue of the week on Saturday night, which is to say Sunday morning, after the custom of a London paper. This was a great convenience, for immediately after the paper was put to bed, the dawn would lower the thermometer from 96° to almost 84° for half an hour, and in that chill—you have no idea how cold is 84° on the grass until you begin to pray for it—a very tired man could set off to sleep ere the heat roused him.

One Saturday night it was my pleasant duty to put the paper to bed alone. A King or courtier or a courtesan or a community was going to die or get a new Constitution, or do something that was important on the other side of the world, and the paper was to be held open till the latest possible minute in order to catch the telegram. It was a pitchy black night, as stifling as a June night can be, and the *loo,* the red-hot wind from the westward, was booming among the tinder-dry trees and pretending that the rain was on its heels. Now and again a spot of almost boiling water would fall on the dust with the flop of a frog, but all our weary world knew that was only pretense. It was a shade cooler in the press-room than the office, so I sat there, while the type ticked and clicked, and the night-jars hooted at the windows, and the all but naked compositors wiped the sweat from their foreheads and called for water. The thing that was keeping us back, whatever it was, would not come off, though the *loo* dropped and the last type was set, and the whole round earth stood still in the choking heat, with its finger on its lips to wait the event. I drowsed, and wondered whether the telegraph was a blessing, and whether this dying man, or struggling people, was aware of the inconvenience the delay was causing. There was no special reason beyond the heat and worry to make tension, but, as the clock-hands crept up to three o'clock and the machines spun their fly-wheels two and three times to see that all was in order, before I said the word that would set them off, I could have shrieked aloud.

Then the roar and rattle of the wheels shivered the quiet into little bits. I rose to go away, but two men in white clothes stood in front of me. The first one said:—"It's him!" The second said:—"So it is!" And they both laughed almost as loudly as the machinery roared, and mopped their foreheads. "We see there was a light burning across the road and we were sleeping in that ditch there for coolness, and I said to my friend here, 'The office is open. Let's come along and speak to him as turned us back from the Degumber State,' " said the smaller of the two. He was the man I had met in the Mhow train, and his fellow was the red-bearded man of Marwar Junction. There was no mistaking the eyebrows of the one or the beard of the other.

I was not pleased, because I wished to go to sleep, not to squabble with loafers. "What do you want?" I asked.

"Half an hour's talk with you cool and comfortable, in the office," said the red-bearded man. "We'd like some drink—the Contrack doesn't begin yet, Peachey, so you needn't look—but what we really want is advice. We don't want money. We ask you as a favor, because you did us a bad turn about Degumber."

I led from the press-room to the stifling office with the maps on the walls, and the red-haired man rubbed his hands. "That's something like," said he. "This was the proper shop to come to. Now, Sir, let me introduce to you Brother Peachey Carnehan, that's him, and Brother Daniel Dravot, that is me, and the less said about our professions the better, for we have been most things in our time. Soldier, sailor, compositor, photographer, proof-reader, street-preacher, and correspondents of the *Backwoodsman* when we thought the paper wanted one. Carnehan is sober, and so am I. Look at us first and see that's sure. It will save you cutting into my talk. We'll take one of your cigars apiece, and you shall see us light."

I watched the test. The men were absolutely sober, so I gave them each a tepid peg.

"Well and good," said Carnehan of the eye-brows, wiping the froth from his mustache. "Let me talk now, Dan. We have been all over India, mostly on foot. We have been boiler-fitters, engine-drivers, petty contractors, and all that, and we have decided that India isn't big enough for such as us."

They certainly were too big for the office. Dravot's beard seemed to fill half the room and Carnehan's shoulders the other half, as they sat on the big table. Carnehan continued:—"The country isn't half worked out because they that govern it won't let you touch it. They spend all their blessed time in governing it, and you can't lift a spade, nor chip a rock, nor look for oil, nor anything like that without all the Government saying—'Leave it alone and let us govern.' Therefore, such as it is, we will let it alone, and go away to some other place where a man isn't crowded and can come to his own. We are not little men, and there is nothing that we are afraid of except Drink, and we have signed a Contrack on that. Therefore, we are going away to be Kings."

"Kings in our own right," muttered Dravot.

"Yes, of course," I said. "You've been tramping in the sun, and it's a very warm night, and hadn't you better sleep over the notion? Come to-morrow."

"Neither drunk nor sunstruck," said Dravot. "We have slept over the notion half a year, and require to see Books and Atlases, and we have decided that there is only one place now in the world that two strong men can Sar-a-*whack*. They call it Kafiristan. By my reckoning it's the top right-hand corner of Afghanistan, not more than three hundred miles from Peshawar. They have two and thirty heathen idols there, and we'll be the thirty-third. It's a mountaineous country, and the women of those parts are very beautiful."

"But that is provided against in the Contrack," said Carnehan. "Neither Women nor Liqu-or, Daniel."

"And that's all we know, except that no one has gone there, and they fight and in any place where they fight a man who knows how to drill men can

always be a King. We shall go to those parts and
say to any King we find—'D' you want to van-
quish your foes?' and we will show him how to
drill men; for that we know better than anything
else. Then we will subvert that King and seize his
Throne and establish a Dy-nasty."

"You'll be cut to pieces before you're fifty miles
across the Border," I said. "You have to travel
through Afghanistan to get to that country. It's
one mass of mountains and peaks and glaciers, and
no Englishman has been through it. The people
are utter brutes, and even if you reached them you
couldn't do anything."

"That's more like," said Carnehan. "If you
could think us a little more mad we would be more
pleased. We have come to you to know about this
country, to read a book about it, and to be shown
maps. We want you to tell us that we are fools
and to show us your books." He turned to the
bookcases.

"Are you at all in earnest?" I said.

"A little," said Dravot sweetly. "As big a map
as you have got, even if it's all blank where Kafiristan is, and any books you've got. We can
read, though we aren't very educated."

I uncased the big thirty-two-miles-to-the-inch
map of India, and the two smaller frontier maps,
hauled down volume INF-KAN of the Encyclopædia Britannica, and the men consulted them.

"See here!" said Dravot, his thumb on the map.
"Up to Jagdallak, Peachey and me know the road

We was there with Roberts's Army. We'll have to turn off to the right at Jagdallak through Laghmann territory. Then we get among the hills— fourteen thousand feet—fifteen thousand—it will be cold work there, but it don't look very far on the map."

I handed him Wood on the Sources of the Oxus. Carnehan was deep in the Encyclopædia.

"They're a mixed lot," said Dravot reflectively; "and it won't help us to know the names of their tribes. The more tribes the more they'll fight, and the better for us. From Jagdallak to Ashang. H'mm!"

"But all the information about the country is as sketchy and inaccurate as can be," I protested. "No one knows anything about it really. Here's the file of the United Services' Institute. Read what Bellew says."

"Blow Bellew!" said Carnehan. "Dan, they're an all-fired lot of heathens, but this book here says they think they're related to us English."

I smoked while the men pored over Raverty, Wood, the maps and the Encyclopædia.

"There is no use your waiting," said Dravot politely. "It's about four o'clock now. We'll go before six o'clock if you want to sleep, and we won't steal any of the papers. Don't you sit up. We're two harmless lunatics, and if you come, to-morrow evening, down to the Serai, we'll say good-by to you."

"You are two fools," I answered. "You'll be

turned back at the Frontier or cut up the minute you set foot in Afghanistan. Do you want any money or a recommendation down-country? I can help you to the chance of work next week."

"Next week we shall be hard at work ourselves, thank you," said Dravot. "It isn't so easy being a King as it looks. When we've got our Kingdom in going order we'll let you know, and you can come up and help us to govern it."

"Would two lunatics make a Contrack like that?" said Carnehan, with subdued pride, showing me a greasy half-sheet of note-paper on which was written the following. I copied it, then and there, as a curiosity:—

This Contract between me and you persuing witnesseth in the name of God—Amen and so forth.

(One) That me and you will settle this matter together:
    i.e., to be Kings of Kafiristan.

(Two) That you and me will not, while this matter is is being settled, look at any Liquor, nor any Woman black, white or brown, so as to get mixed up with one or the other harmful.

(Three) That we conduct ourselves with dignity and discretion, and if one of us gets into trouble the other will stay by him.

    Signed by you and me this day.
      Peachey Taliaferro Carnehan.
      Daniel Dravot.
      Both Gentlemen at Large.

"There was no need for the last article," said Carnehan, blushing modestly; "but it looks regular. Now you know the sort of men that loafers are—we are loafers, Dan, until we get out of India—and do you think that we would sign a Contrack like that unless we was in earnest? We have kept away from the two things that make life worth having."

"You won't enjoy your lives much longer if you are going to try this idiotic adventure. Don't set the office on fire," I said, "and go away before nine o'clock."

I left them still poring over the maps and making notes on the back of the "Contrack." "Be sure to come down to the Serai to-morrow," were their parting words.

The Kumharsen Serai is the great four-square sink of humanity where the strings of camels and horses from the North load and unload. All the nationalities of Central Asia may be found there, and most of the folk of India proper. Balkh and Bokhara there meet Bengal and Bombay, and try to draw eye-teeth. You can buy ponies, turquoises, Persian pussy-cats, saddle-bags, fat-tailed sheep and musk in the Kumharsen Serai, and get many strange things for nothing. In the afternoon I went down there to see whether my friends intended to keep their word or were lying about drunk.

A priest attired in fragments of ribbons and rags stalked up to me, gravely twisting a child's paper whirligig. Behind him was his servant bending under the load of a crate of mud toys. The two were loading up two camels, and the inhabitants of the Serai watched them with shrieks of laughter.

"The priest is mad," said a horse-dealer to me. "He is going up to Kabul to sell toys to the Amir. He will either be raised to honor or have his head cut off. He came in here this morning and has been behaving madly ever since."

"The witless are under the protection of God," stammered a flat-cheeked Usbeg in broken Hindi. "They foretell future events."

"Would they could have foretold that my caravan would have been cut up by the Shinwaris almost within shadow of the Pass!" grunted the Eusufzai agent of a Rajputana trading-house whose goods had been feloniously diverted into the hands of other robbers just across the Border, and whose misfortunes were the laughing-stock of the bazaar. "Ohé, priest, whence come you and whither do you go?"

"From Roum have I come," shouted the priest, waving his whirligig; "from Roum, blown by the breath of a hundred devils across the sea! O thieves, robbers, liars, the blessing of Pir Khan on pigs, dogs, and perjurers! Who will take the Protected of God to the North to sell charms that are never still to the Amir? The camels shall not gall, the sons shall not fall sick, and the wives shall remain faithful while they are away, of the men who give me place in their caravan. Who will assist me to slipper the King of Roos with a golden slipper with a silver heel? The protection

of Pir Khan be upon his labors!" He spread out
the skirts of his gaberdine and pirouetted between
the lines of tethered horses.

"There starts a caravan from Peshawar to
Kabul in twenty days, *Huzrut*," said the Eusufzai
trader. "My camels go therewith. Do thou also
go and bring us good luck."

"I will go even now!" shouted the priest. "I
will depart upon my winged camels, and be at
Peshawar in a day! Ho! Hazar Mir Khan," he
yelled to his servant, "drive out the camels, but
let me first mount my own."

He leaped on the back of his beast as it knelt,
and, turning round to me, cried:—"Come thou
also, Sahib, a little along the road, and I will sell
thee a charm—an amulet that shall make thee
King of Kafiristan."

Then the light broke upon me, and I followed
the two camels out of the Serai till we reached
open road and the priest halted.

"What d'you think o' that?" said he in English.
"Carnehan can't talk their patter, so I've made
him my servant. He makes a handsome servant.
'Tisn't for nothing that I've been knocking about
the country for fourteen years. Didn't I do that
talk neat? We'll hitch on to a caravan at Peshawar till we get to Jagdallak, and then we'll see if
we can get donkeys for our camels, and strike into
Kafiristan. Whirligigs for the Amir, O Lor!
Put your hand under the camel-bags and tell me
what you feel."

I felt the butt of a Martini, and another and another.

"Twenty of 'em," said Dravot placidly. "Twenty of 'em, and ammunition to correspond, under the whirligigs and the mud dolls."

"Heaven help you if you are caught with those things!" I said. "A Martini is worth her weight in silver among the Pathans."

"Fifteen hundred rupees of capital—every rupee we could beg, borrow, or steal—are invested on these two camels," said Dravot. "We won't get caught. We're going through the Khaiber with a regular caravan. Who'd touch a poor mad priest?"

"Have you got everything you want?" I asked, overcome with astonishment.

"Not yet, but we shall soon. Give us a memento of your kindness, Brother. You did me a service yesterday, and that time in Marwar. Half my Kingdom shall you have, as the saying is." I slipped a small charm compass from my watch-chain and handed it up to the priest.

"Good-by," said Dravot, giving me hand cautiously. "It's the last time we'll shake hands with an Englishman these many days. Shake hands with him Carnehan," he cried, as the second camel passed me.

Carnehan leaned down and shook hands. Then the camels passed away along the dusty road, and I was left alone to wonder. My eye could detect no failure in the disguises. The scene in the Serai attested that they were complete to the native mind. There was just the chance, therefore, that Carnehan and Dravot would be able to wander through Afghanistan without detection. But, beyond, they would find death, certain and awful death.

Ten days later a native friend of mine, giving me the news of the day from Peshawar, wound up his letter with:—"There has been much laughter here on account of a certain mad priest who is going on his estimation to sell pretty gauds and insignificant trinkets which he ascribes as great charms to H. H. the Amir of Bokhara. He passed through Peshawar and associated himself to the Second Summer caravan that goes to Kabul. The merchants are pleased because through superstition they imagine that such mad fellows bring good-fortune."

The two, then, were beyond the Border. I would have prayed for them, but, that night, a real King died in Europe, and demanded an obituary notice.

.   .   .   .

The wheel of the world swings through the same phases again and again. Summer passed and winter thereafter, and came and passed again. The daily paper continued and I with it, and upon the third summer there fell a hot night, a night-issue, and a strained waiting for something to be telegraphed from the other side of the world, exactly as had happened before. A few great men had died in the past two years, the machines worked with more clatter, and some of the trees in the Office garden were a few feet taller. But that was all the difference.

I passed over to the press-room, and went through just such a scene as I have already described. The nervous tension was stronger than it had been two years before, and I felt the heat more acutely. At three o'clock I cried, "Print off," and turned to go, when there crept to my chair what was left of a man. He was bent into a circle, his head was sunk between his shoulders, and he moved his feet one over the other like a bear. I could hardly see whether he walked or crawled—this rag-wrapped, whining cripple who addressed me by name, crying that he was come back. "Can you give me a drink?" he whimpered. "For the Lord's sake, give me a drink!"

I went back to the office, the man following with groans of pain, and I turned up the lamp.

"Don't you know me?" he gasped, dropping into a chair, and he turned his drawn face, surmounted by a shock of gray hair, to the light.

I looked at him intently. Once before had I seen eyebrows that met over the nose in an inch-broad black band, but for the life of me I could not tell where.

"I don't know you," I said, handing him the whisky. "What can I do for you?"

He took a gulp of the spirit raw, and shivered in spite of the suffocating heat.

"I've come back," he repeated; "and I was the King of Kafiristan—me and Dravot—crowned Kings we was! In this office we settled it—you setting there and giving us the books. I am Peachey—Peachey Taliaferro Carnehan, and you've been setting here ever since—O Lord!"

I was more than a little astonished, and expressed my feelings accordingly.

"It's true," said Carnehan, with a dry cackle, nursing his feet, which were wrapped in rags. "True as gospel. Kings we were, with crowns upon our heads—me and Dravot—poor Dan—oh, poor, poor Dan, that would never take advice, not though I begged of him!"

"Take the whisky," I said, "and take your own time. Tell me all you can recollect of everything from beginning to end. You got across the border on your camels, Dravot dressed as a mad priest and you his servant. Do you remember that?"

"I ain't mad—yet, but I shall be that way soon. Of course I remember. Keep looking at me, or maybe my words will go all to pieces. Keep looking at me in my eyes and don't say anything."

I leaned forward and looked into his face as steadily as I could. He dropped one hand upon the table and I grasped it by the wrist. It was twisted like a bird's claw, and upon the back was a ragged, red, diamond-shaped scar.

"No, don't look there. Look at me," said Carnehan.

"That comes afterwards, but for the Lord's sake don't distrack me. We left with that caravan, me and Dravot, playing all sorts of antics to amuse the people we were with. Dravot used to make us laugh in the evenings when all the people was cooking their dinners—cooking their dinners, and . . . what did they do then? They lit little fires with sparks that went into Dravot's beard, and we all laughed—fit to die. Little red fires they was, going into Dravot's big red beard—so funny." His eyes left mine and he smiled foolishly.

"You went as far as Jagdallak with that caravan," I said at a venture, "after you had lit those fires. To Jagdallak, where you turned off to try to get into Kafiristan."

"No, we didn't neither. What are you talking about? We turned off before Jagdallak, because we heard the roads was good. But they wasn't good enough for our two camels—mine and Dravot's. When we left the caravan, Dravot took off all his clothes and mine too, and said we would be heathen, because the Kafirs didn't allow Mohammedans to talk to them. So we dressed betwixt and between, and such a sight as Daniel Dravot I never saw yet nor expect to see again. He burned half his beard, and slung a sheepskin over his shoulder, and shaved his head into patterns. He shaved mine, too, and made me wear outrageous things to look like a heathen. That was in a most mountaineous country, and our camels couldn't go along any more because of the mountains. They were tall and black, and coming home I saw them fight like wild goats—there are lots of goats in Kafiristan. And these mountains, they never keep still, no more than the goats. Always fighting they are, and don't let you sleep at night."

"Take some more whisky," I said very slowly. "What did you and Daniel Dravot do when the camels could go no further because of the rough roads that led into Kafiristan?"

"What did which do? There was a party called Peachey Taliaferro Carnehan that was with Dravot. Shall I tell you about him? He died out there in the cold. Slap from the bridge fell old Peachey, turning and twisting in the air like a penny whirligig that you can sell to the Amir.—No; they was two or three ha'pence, those whirligigs, or I am much mistaken and woeful sore. And then these camels were no use, and Peachey said to Dravot—'For the Lord's sake, let's get out of this before our heads are chopped off,' and with that they killed the camels all among the mountains, not having anything in particular to eat, but first they took off the boxes with the guns and the ammunition, and two men came along driving four mules. Dravot up and dances in front of them, singing,—'Sell me four mules.' Says the first man,—'If you are rich enough to buy you are rich enough to rob;' but before ever he could put his hand to his knife, Dravot breaks his neck over his knee, and the other party runs away. So Carnehan loaded the mules with the rifles that was taken off the camels, and together we starts forward into those bitter cold mountaineous parts, and never a road broader than the back of your hand."

He paused for a moment, while I asked him if he could remember the nature of the country through which he had journeyed.

"I am telling you as straight as I can, but my head isn't as good as it might be. They drove nails through it to make me hear better how Dravot died. The country was mountaineous and the mules were most contrary, and the inhabitants was dispersed and solitary. They went up and up, and down and down, and that other party, Carnehan, was imploring of Dravot not to sing and whistle so loud, for fear of bringing down the tremenjus avalanches. But Dravot says that if a King couldn't sing it wasn't worth being a King, and whacked the mules over the rump, and never took no heed for ten cold days. We came to a big level valley all among the mountains, and the mules were near dead, so we killed them, not having anything in special for them or us to eat. We sat upon the boxes, and played odd and even with the cartridges that was jolted out.

"Then ten men with bows and arrows ran down that valley, chasing twenty men with bows and

arrows, and the row was tremenjus. They was
fair men—fairer than you or me—with yellow
hair and remarkable well built. Says Dravot, un-
packing the guns—'This is the beginning of the
business. We'll fight for the ten men,' and with
that he fires two rifles at the twenty men, and
drops one of them at two hundred yards from the
rock where we was sitting. The other men began
to run, but Carnehan and Dravot sits on the boxes
picking them off at all ranges, up and down the
valley. Then we goes up to the ten men that had
run across the snow too, and they fires a footy
little arrow at us. Dravot he shoots above their
heads and they all falls down flat. Then he walks
over them and kicks them, and then he lifts them
up and shakes hands all round to make them
friendly like. He calls them and gives them the
boxes to carry, and waves his hand for all the
world as though he was King already. They
takes the boxes and him across the valley and up
the hill into a pine wood on the top, where there
was half a dozen big stone idols. Dravot he goes
to the biggest—a fellow they call Imbra—and lays
a rifle and a cartridge at his feet, rubbing his nose
respectful with his own nose, patting him on the
head, and saluting in front of it. He turns round
to the men and nods his head, and says,—'That's
all right. I'm in the know too, and all these old
jim-jams are my friends.' Then he opens his
mouth and points down it, and when the first man
brings him food, he says—'No'; and when the

second man brings him food, he says—'No'; but when one of the old priests and the boss of the village brings him food, he says—'Yes'; very haughty, and eats it slow. That was how we came to our first village, without any trouble, just as though we had tumbled from the skies. But we tumbled from one of those damned rope-bridges, you see, and you couldn't expect a man to laugh much after that."

"Take some more whisky and go on," I said. "That was the first village you came into. How did you get to be king!"

"I wasn't King," said Carnehan. "Dravot he was the King, and a handsome man he looked with the gold crown on his head and all. Him and the other party stayed in that village, and every morning Dravot sat by the side of old Imbra, and the people came and worshiped. That was Dravot's order. Then a lot of men came into the valley, and Carnehan and Dravot picks them off with the rifles before they knew where they was, and runs down into the valley and up again the other side, and finds another village, same as the first one, and the people all falls down flat on their faces, and Dravot says,—'Now what is the trouble between you two villages?' and the people points to a woman, as fair as you or me, that was carried off, and Dravot takes her back to the first village and counts up the dead—eight there was. For each dead man Dravot pours a little milk on the ground and waves his arms like a whirligig and 'That's all right,' says he. Then he and Carnehan takes the big boss of each village by the arm and walks them down into the valley, and shows them how to scratch a line with a spear right down the valley, and gives each a sod of turf from both sides o' the line. Then all the people comes down and shouts like the devil and all, and Dravot says,—'Go and dig the land, and be fruitful and multiply,' which they did, though they didn't understand. Then we asks the names of things in their lingo—bread and water and fire and idols and such, and Dravot leads the priest of each village up to the idol, and says he must sit there and judge the people, and if anything goes wrong he is to be shot.

"Next week they was all turning up the land in the valley as quiet as bees and much prettier, and the priests heard all the complaints and told Dravot in dumb show what it was about. 'That's just the beginning,' says Dravot. 'They think we're Gods.' He and Carnehan picks out twenty good men and shows them how to click off a rifle, and form fours, and advance in line, and they was very pleased to do so, and clever to see the hang of it. Then he takes out his pipe and his baccy-pouch and leaves one at one village, and one at the other and off we two goes to see what was to be done in the next valley. That was all rock, and there was a little village there, and Carnehan says,—'Send 'em to the old valley to plant,' and takes 'em there and gives 'em some land that wasn't took before. They were a poor lot, and we blooded 'em with a kid before letting 'em into the new Kingdom. That was to impress the people, and then they settled down quiet, and Carnehan went back to Dravot who had got into another valley, all snow and ice and most mountaineous. There was no people there and the Army got afraid, so Dravot shoots one of them, and goes on till he finds some people in a village, and the Army explains that unless the people wants to be killed they had better not shoot their little matchlocks; for they had matchlocks. We makes friends with the priest and I stays there alone with two of the Army, teaching the men how to drill, and a thundering big Chief comes across the snow with kettledrums and horns twanging, because he heard there was a new God kicking about. Carnehan sights for the brown of the men half a mile across the snow and wings one of them. Then he sends a message to the Chief that, unless he wished to be killed, he must come and shake hands with me and leave his arms behind. The Chief comes alone first, and Carnehan shakes hands with him and whirls his arms about, same as Dravot used, and very much surprised that Chief was, and strokes my eyebrows. Then Carnehan goes alone to the Chief, and asks him in dumb show if he had an enemy he hated. 'I have,' says the Chief. So Carnehan weeds out the pick of his men, and sets the two of the Army to show them drill and at the end of

two weeks the men can maneuver about as well
as Volunteers. So he marches with the Chief to
a great big plain on the top of a mountain, and
the Chief's men rushes into a village and takes
it; we three Martinis firing into the brown of the
enemy. So we took that village too, and I gives
the Chief a rag from my coat and says, 'Occupy
till I come;' which was scriptural. By way of a
reminder, when me and the Army was eighteen
hundred yards away, I drops a bullet near him
standing on the snow, and all the people falls flat
on their faces. Then I sends a letter to Dravot,
wherever he be by land or by sea."

At the risk of throwing the creature out of train
I interrupted,—"How could you write a letter up
yonder?"

"The letter?—Oh!—The letter! Keep looking
at me between the eyes, please. It was a string-
talk letter, that we'd learned the way of it from a
blind beggar in the Punjab."

I remember that there had once come to the
office a blind man with a knotted twig and a piece
of string which he wound round the twig according to some cipher of his own. He could, after
the lapse of days and hours, repeat the sentence
which he had reeled up. He had reduced the
alphabet to eleven primitive sounds; and tried to
teach me his method, but failed.

"I sent that letter to Dravot," said Carnehan;
"and told him to come back because this Kingdom
was growing too big for me to handle, and then I

struck for the first valley, to see how the priests
were working. They called the village we took
along with the Chief, Bashkai, and the first village
we took, Er-Heb. The priests at Er-Heb was
doing all right, but they had a lot of pending cases
about land to show me, and some men from another village had been firing arrows at night. I
went out and looked for that village and fired four
rounds at it from a thousand yards. That used
all the cartridges I cared to spend, and I waited
for Dravot, who had been away two or three
months, and I kept my people quiet.

"One morning I heard the devil's own noise of
drums and horns, and Dan Dravot marches down
the hill with his Army and a tail of hundreds of
men, and,—which was the most amazing—a great
gold crown on his head. 'My Gord, Carnehan,'
says Daniel, 'this is a tremenjus business, and
we've got the whole country as far as it's worth
having. I am the son of Alexander by Queen
Semiramis, and you're my younger brother and a
God too! It's the biggest thing we've ever seen.
I've been marching and fighting for six weeks
with the Army, and every footy little village for
fifty miles has come in rejoiceful; and more than
that, I've got the key of the whole show, as you'll
see, and I've got a crown for you! I told 'em to
make two of 'em at a place called Shu, where the
gold lies in the rock like suet in mutton. Gold
I've seen and turquoise I've kicked out of the cliffs,
and there's garnets in the sands of the river, and

here's a chunk of amber that a man brought me. Call up all the priests and, here, take your crown.'

"One of the men opens a black hair bag and I slips the crown on. It was too small and too heavy, but I wore it for the glory. Hammered gold it was—five pound weight, like a hoop of a barrel.

" 'Peachey,' says Dravot, 'we don't want to fight no more. The Craft's the trick so help me!' and he brings forward that same Chief that I left at Bashkai—Billy Fish we called him afterwards, because he was so like Billy Fish that drove the big tank-engine at Mach on the Bolan in the old days. 'Shake hands with him,' says Dravot, and I shook hands and nearly dropped, for Billy Fish gave me the Grip. I said nothing, but tried him with the Fellow Craft Grip. He answers, all right, and I tried the Master's Grip, but that was a slip. 'A Fellow Craft he is!' I says to Dan. 'Does he know the word?' 'He does,' says Dan, 'and all the priests know. It's a miracle! The Chiefs and the priests can work a Fellow Craft Lodge in a way that's very like ours, and they've cut the marks on the rocks, but they don't know the Third Degree, and they've come to find out. It's Gord's Truth. I've known these long years that the Afghans knew up to the Fellow Craft Degree, but this is a miracle. A God and a Grand-Master of the Craft am I, and a Lodge in the Third Degree I will open, and we'll raise the head priests and the Chiefs of the villages.'

" 'It's against all the law,' I says, 'holding a
Lodge without warrant from any one; and we
never held office in any Lodge.'

" 'It's a master-stroke of policy,' says Dravot.
'It means running the country as easy as a four-
wheeled bogy on a down grade. We can't stop to
inquire now, or they'll turn against us. I've forty
Chiefs at my heel, and passed and raised according
to their merit they shall be. Billet these men on
the villages and see that we run up a Lodge of
some kind. The temple of Imbra will do for the
Lodge-room. The women must make aprons as
you show them. I'll hold a levee of Chiefs to-
night and Lodge to-morrow.'

"I was fair run off my legs, but I wasn't such
a fool as not to see what a pull this Craft business gave us. I showed the priests' families how
to make aprons of the degrees, but for Dravot's
apron the blue border and marks was made of
turquoise lumps on white hide, not cloth. We
took a great square stone in the temple for the
Master's chair, and little stones for the officers'
chairs, and painted the black pavement with white
squares, and did what we could to make things
regular.

"At the levee which was held that night on the
hillside with big bonfires, Dravot gives out that
him and me were Gods and sons of Alexander, and
Past Grand-Masters in the Craft, and was come
to make Kafiristan a country where every man
should eat in peace and drink in quiet, and specially

obey us. Then the Chiefs come round to shake
hands, and they was so hairy and white and fair
it was just like shaking hands with old friends.
We gave them names according as they was like
men we had known in India—Billy Fish, Holly
Dilworth, Pikky Kergan that was Bazar-master
when I was at Mhow, and so on and so on.

"The most amazing miracle was at Lodge next
night. One of the old priests was watching us
continuous, and I felt uneasy, for I knew we'd
have to fudge the Ritual, and I didn't know what
the men knew. The old priest was a stranger
come in from beyond the village of Bashkai. The
minute Dravot puts on the Master's apron that
the girls had made for him, the priest fetches a
whoop and a howl, and tries to overturn the stone
that Dravot was sitting on. 'It's all up now,' I
says. 'That comes of meddling with the Craft
without warrant!' Dravot never winked an eye,
not when ten priests took and tilted over the
Grand-Master's chair—which was to say the stone
of Imbra. The priest begins rubbing the bottom
end of it to clear away the black dirt, and presently he shows all the other priests the Master's
Mark, same as was on Dravot's apron, cut into
the stone. Not even the priests of the temple of
Imbra knew it was there. The old chap falls flat
on his face at Dravot's feet and kisses 'em. 'Luck
again,' says Dravot, across the Lodge to me, 'they
say it's the missing Mark that no one could understand the why of. We're more than safe now.'

Then he bangs the butt of his gun for a gavel and says:—'By virtue of the authority vested in me by my own right hand and the help of Peachey, I declare myself Grand-Master of all Free-masonry in Kafiristan in this the Mother Lodge o' the country, and King of Kafiristan equally with Peachey!' At that he puts on his crown and I puts on mine—I was doing Senior Warden —and we opens the Lodge in most ample form. It was a amazing miracle! The priests moved in Lodge through the first two degrees almost without telling, as if the memory was coming back to them. After that, Peachey and Dravot raised such as was worthy—high priests and Chiefs of far-off villages. Billy Fish was the first, and I can tell you we scared the soul out of him. It was not in any way according to Ritual, but it served our turn. We didn't raise more than ten of the biggest men because we didn't want to make the Degree common. And they was clamoring to be raised.

" 'In another six months,' says Dravot, "we'll hold another Communication and see how you are working.' Then he asks them about their villages, and learns that they was fighting one against the other and were fair sick and tired of it. And when they wasn't doing that they was fighting with the Mohammedans. 'You can fight those when they come into our country,' says Dravot. 'Tell off every tenth man of your tribes for a Frontier guard, and send two hundred at a time to this valley to be drilled. Nobody is going to be shot or speared any more so long as he does well, and I know that you won't cheat me because you're white people—sons of Alexander—and not like common, black Mohammedans. You are my people and by God,' says he, running off into English at the end—'I'll make a damned fine Nation of you, or I'll die in the making.'

"I can't tell all we did for the next six months because Dravot did a lot I couldn't see the hang of, and he learned their lingo in a way I never could. My work was to help the people plow, and now and again go out with some of the Army and see what the other villages were doing, and make 'em throw rope-bridges across the ravines which cut up the country horrid. Dravot was very kind to me, but when he walked up and down in the pine wood, pulling that bloody red beard of his with both fists, I knew he was thinking plans I could not advise him about, and I just waited for orders.

"But Dravot never showed me disrespect before the people. They were afraid of me and the Army, but they loved Dan. He was the best of friends with the priests and the Chiefs; but any one could come across the hills with a complaint and Dravot would hear him out fair, and call four priests together and say what was to be done. He used to call in Billy Fish from Bashkai, and Pikky Kergan from Shu, and an old Chief we called Kafuzelum—it was like enough to his real name—and hold councils with 'em when there was

any fighting to be done in small villages. That
was his Council of War, and the four priests of
Bashkai, Shu, Khawak, and Madora was his
Privy Council. Between the lot of 'em they sent
me, with forty men and twenty rifles, and sixty
men carrying turquoises, into the Ghorband country to buy those hand-made Martini rifles, that
come out of the Amir's workshops at Kabul, from
one of the Amir's Herati regiments that would
have sold the very teeth out of their mouths for
turquoises.

"I stayed in Ghorband a month, and gave the
Governor there the pick of my baskets for hush-
money, and bribed the Colonel of the regiment
some more, and, between the two and the tribes-
people, we got more than a hundred hand-made
Martinis, a hundred good Kohat Jezails that'll
throw to six hundred yards, and forty man-loads
of very bad ammunition for the rifles. I came
back with what I had, and distributed 'em among
the men that the Chiefs sent in to me to drill.
Dravot was too busy to attend to these things,
but the old Army that we first made helped me,
and we turned out five hundred men that could
drill, and two hundred that knew how to hold arms
pretty straight. Even those cork-screwed, hand-
made guns was a miracle to them. Dravot talked
big about powder-shops and factories, walking up
and down in the pine wood when the winter was
coming on.

" 'I won't make a Nation,' says he. 'I'll make

an Empire! These men aren't niggers; they're English! Look at their eyes—look at their mouths. Look at the way they stand up. They sit on chairs in their own houses. They're the Lost Tribes, or something like it, and they've grown to be English. I'll take a census in the spring if the priests don't get frightened. There must be a fair two million of 'em in these hills. The villages are full o' little children. Two million people—two hundred and fifty thousand fighting men—and all English! They only want the rifles and a little drilling. Two hundred and fifty thousand men, ready to cut in on Russia's right flank when she tries for India! Peachey, man,' he says, chewing his beard in great hunks, 'we shall be Emperors—Emperors of the Earth! Rajah Brooke will be a suckling to us. I'll treat the Viceroy on equal terms. I'll ask him to send me twelve picked English—twelve that I know of—to help us govern a bit. There's Mackray, Sergeant-pensioner at Segowli—many's the good dinner he's given me, and his wife a pair of trousers. There's Donkin, the Warder of Toung-hoo Jail; there's hundreds that I could lay my hand on if I was in India. The Viceroy shall do it for me. I'll send a man through in the spring for those men, and I'll write for a dispensation from the Grand Lodge for what I've done as Grand-Master. That—and all the Sniders that'll be thrown out when the native troops in India take up the Martini. They'll be worn smooth, but they'll do for fighting in these hills. Twelve English, a hundred thousand Sniders run through the Amir's country in driblets—I'd be content with twenty thousand in one year—and we'd be an Empire. When everything was ship-shape, I'd hand over the crown—this crown I'm wearing now—to Queen Victoria on my knees, and she'd say:—"Rise up, Sir Daniel Dravot." Oh, it's big! It's big, I tell you! But there's so much to be done in every place—Bashkai, Khawk, Shu, and everywhere else.'

" 'What is it?' I says. 'There are no more men coming in to be drilled this autumn. Look at those fat, black clouds. They're bringing the snow.'

" 'It isn't that,' says Daniel, putting his hand very hard on my shoulder; 'and I don't wish to say anything that's against you, for no other living man would have followed me and made me what I am as you have done. You're a first-class Commander-in-Chief, and the people know you; but—it's a big country, and somehow you can't help me, Peachy, in the way I want to be helped.'

" 'Go to your blasted priests, then!' I said, and I was sorry when I made that remark, but it did hurt to find Daniel talking so superior when I'd drilled all the men, and done all he told me.

" 'Don't let's quarrel, Peachey,' says Daniel without cursing. 'You're a King too, and the half of this Kingdom is yours; but can't you see, Peachey, we want cleverer men than us now—

three or four of 'em that we can scatter about for our Deputies. It's a hugeous great State, and I can't always tell the right thing to do, and I haven't time for all I want to do, and here's the winter coming on and all.' He put half his beard into his mouth, and it was as red as the gold of his crown.

" 'I'm sorry Daniel,' says I. 'I've done all I could. I've drilled the men and shown the people how to stack their oats better; and I've brought in those tinware rifles from Ghorband—but I know what you're driving at. I take it Kings always feel oppressed that way.'

" 'There's another thing too,' says Dravot, walking up and down. 'The winter's coming and these people won't be giving much trouble, and if they do we can't move about. I want a wife.'

" 'For Gord's sake leave the women alone!' I says. 'We've both got all the work we can, though I am a fool. Remember the Contrack, and keep clear o' women.'

" 'The Contrack only lasted till such time as we was Kings; and Kings we have been these months past,' says Dravot, weighing his crown in his hand. 'You go get a wife too, Peachey—a nice, strappin', plump girl that'll keep you warm in the winter. They're prettier than English girls, and we can take the pick of 'em. Boil 'em once or twice in hot water, and they'll come as fair as chicken and ham.'

" 'Don't tempt me!' I says. 'I will not have

any dealings with a woman not till we are a dam' site more settled than we are now. I've been doing the work o' two men, and you've been doing the work o' three. Let's lie off a bit, and see if we can get some better tobacco from Afghan country and run in some good liquor; but no women.'

" 'Who's talking o' women?' says Dravot, 'I said wife—a Queen to breed a King's son for the King. A Queen out of the strongest tribe, that'll make them your blood-brothers, and that'll lie by your side and tell you all the people thinks about you and their own affairs. That's what I want.'

" 'Do you remember that Bengali woman I kept at Mogul Serai when I was a plate-layer?' says I. 'A fat lot o' good she was to me. She taught me the lingo and one or two other things; out what happened? She ran away with the Station Master's servant and half my month's pay. Then she turned up at Dadur Junction in tow of a half-caste, and had the impidence to say I was her husband—all among the drivers in the running shed!'

" 'We're done with that,' says Dravot. 'These women are whiter than you or me, and a Queen I will have for the winter months.'

" 'For the last time o' asking, Dan, do not,' I say. 'It'll only bring us harm. The Bible says that Kings ain't to waste their strength on women, 'specially when they've got a new raw Kingdom to work over.'

" 'For the last time of answering I will,' said Dravot, and he went away through the pine-trees looking like a big red devil. The low sun hit his crown and beard on one side and the two blazed like hot coals.

"But getting a wife was not as easy as Dan thought. He put it before the Council, and there was no answer till Billy Fish said that he'd better ask the girls. Dravot damned them all round. 'What's wrong with me?' he shouts, standing by the idol Imbra. 'Am I a dog or am I not enough of a man for your wenches? Haven't I put the shadow of my hand over this country? Who stopped the last Afghan raid?' It was me really, but Dravot was too angry to remember. 'Who bought your guns? Who repaired the bridges? Who's the Grand-Master of the sign cut in the stone?' and he thumped his hand on the block that he used to sit on in Lodge, and at Council, which opened like Lodge always. Billy Fish said nothing and no more did the others. 'Keep your hair on, Dan,' said I; 'and ask the girls. That's how it's done at Home, and these people are quite English.'

" 'The marriage of the King is a matter of State,' says Dan, in a white-hot rage, for he could feel, I hope, that he was going against his better mind. He walked out of the Council-room, and the others sat still, looking at the ground.

" 'Billy Fish,' says I to the Chief of Bashkai, 'what's the difficulty here? A straight answer to a true friend.' 'You know,' says Billy Fish. 'How should a man tell you who know everything? How can daughters of men marry Gods or Devils? It's not proper.'

"I remembered something like that in the Bible; but if, after seeing us as long as they had, they still believed we were Gods, it wasn't for me to undeceive them.

" 'A God can do anything,' says I. 'If the King is fond of a girl he'll not let her die.' 'She'll have to,' said Billy Fish. 'There are all sorts of Gods and Devils in these mountains, and now and again a girl marries one of them and isn't seen any more. Besides, you two know the Mark cut in the stone. Only the Gods know that. We thought you were men till you showed the sign of the Master.'

"I wished then that we had explained about the loss of the genuine secrets of a Master-Mason at the first go-off; but I said nothing. All that night there was a blowing of horns in a little dark temple half-way down the hill, and I heard a girl crying fit to die. One of the priests told us that she was being prepared to marry the King.

" 'I'll have no nonsense of that kind,' says Dan. 'I don't want to interfere with your customs, but I'll take my own wife.' 'The girl's a little bit afraid,' says the priest. 'She thinks she's going to die, and they are a-heartening of her up down in the temple.'

" 'Hearten her very tender, then,' says Dravot, 'or I'll hearten you with the butt of a gun so

that you'll never want to be heartened again.'
He licked his lips, did Dan, and stayed up walking
about more than half the night, thinking of the
wife that he was going to get in the morning. I
wasn't any means comfortable, for I knew that
dealings with a woman in foreign parts, though
you was a crowned King twenty times over, could
not but be risky. I got up very early in the morning while Dravot was asleep, and I saw the priests
talking together in whispers, and the Chiefs talking together too, and they looked at me out of
the corners of their eyes.

" 'What's up, Fish?" I says to the Bashkai
man, who was wrapped up in his furs and looking
splendid to behold.

" 'I can't rightly say,' says he; 'but if you can
induce the King to drop all this nonsense about
marriage, you'll be doing him and me and yourself a great service.'

" 'That I do believe,' says I. 'But sure, you
know Billy, as well as me, having fought against
and for us, that the King and me are nothing more
than two of the finest men that God Almighty
ever made. Nothing more, I do assure you.'

" 'That may be,' says Billy Fish, 'and yet I
should be sorry if it was.' He sinks his head upon
his great fur cloak for a minute and thinks.
'King,' says he, 'be you man or God or Devil, I'll
stick by you to-day. I have twenty of my men
with me, and they will follow me. We'll go to
Bashkai until the storm blows over.'

"A little snow had fallen in the night, and everything was white except the greasy fat clouds that blew down and down from the north. Dravot came out with his crown on his head, swinging his arms and stamping his feet, and looking more pleased than Punch.

" 'For the last time, drop it, Dan,' says I in a whisper. 'Billy Fish here says that there will be a row.'

" 'A row among my people!' says Dravot. 'Not much. Peachey, you're a fool not to get a wife too. Where's the girl?' says he with a voice as loud as the braying of a jackass. 'Call up all the Chiefs and priests and let the Emperor see if his wife suits him.'

"There was no need to call any one. They were all there leaning on their guns and spears round the clearing in the center of the pine wood. A deputation of priests went down to the little temple to bring up the girl, and the horns blew up fit to wake the dead. Billy Fish saunters round and gets as close to Daniel as he could, and behind him stood his twenty men with matchlocks. Not a man of them under six feet. I was next to Dravot, and behind me was twenty men of the regular Army. Up comes the girl, and a strapping wench she was, covered with silver and turquoises, but white as death, and looking back every minute at the priests.

" 'She'll do,' said Dan, looking her over. 'What's to be afraid of, lass? Come and kiss me.'

He puts his arm round her. She shuts her eyes, gives a bit of a squeak, and down goes her face in the side of Dan's flaming red beard.

" 'The slut's bitten me!' says he, clapping his hand to his neck, and, sure, enough, his hand was red with blood. Billy Fish and two of his matchlock-men catches hold of Dan by the shoulders and drags him into the Bashkai lot, while the priests howls in their lingo,—'Neither God nor Devil but a man!' I was all taken aback, for a priest cut at me in front, and the Army behind began firing into the Bashkai men.

" 'God A-mighty!' says Dan. 'What is the meaning o' this?'

" 'Come back! Come away!' says Billy Fish. 'Ruin and Mutiny is the matter. We'll break for Bashkai if we can.'

"I tried to give some sort of orders to my men —the men o' the regular Army—but it was no use, so I fired into the brown of 'em with an English Martini and drilled three beggars in a line. The valley was full of shouting, howling creatures, and every soul was shrieking 'Not a God nor a Devil but only a man!' The Bashkai troops stuck to Billy Fish all they were worth, but their matchlocks wasn't half as good as the Kabul breech-loaders, and four of them dropped. Dan was bellowing like a bull, for he was very wrathy; and Billy Fish had a hard job to prevent him running out at the crowd.

" 'We can't stand,' says Billy Fish. 'Make a run for it down the valley! The whole place is against us.' The matchlock-men ran, and we went down the valley in spite of Dravot's protestations. He was swearing horribly and crying out that he was a King. The priests rolled great stones on us, and the regular Army fired hard, and there wasn't more than six men, not counting Dan, Billy Fish, and Me, that came down to the bottom of the valley alive.

"Then they stopped firing and the horns in the temple blew again. 'Come away—for Gord's sake come away!' says Billy Fish. 'They'll send runners out to all the villages before ever we get to Bashkai. I can protect you there, but I can't do anything now.'

"My own notion is that Dan began to go mad in his head from that hour. He stared up and down like a stuck pig. Then he was all for walking back alone and killing the priests with his bare hands; which he could have done. 'An Emperor am I,' says Daniel, 'and next year I shall be a Knight of the Queen.'

" 'All right, Dan,' says I; 'but come along now while there's time.'

" 'It's your fault,' says he, 'for not looking after your Army better. There was mutiny in the midst, and you didn't know—you damned engine-driving, plate-laying, missionary's pass-hunting hound!' He sat upon a rock and called me every foul name he could lay tongue to. I was too heart-sick to care though it was all his foolishness that brought the smash.

" 'I'm sorry, Dan,' says I, 'but there's no accounting for natives. This business is our Fifty-Seven. Maybe we'll make something out of it yet, when we've got to Bashkai.'

" 'Let's get to Bashkai, then,' says Dan, 'and, by God, when I come back here again I'll sweep the valley so there isn't a bug in a blanket left!'

"We walked all that day, and all that night Dan was stumping up and down on the snow, chewing his beard and muttering to himself.

" 'There's no hope o' getting clear,' said Billy Fish. 'The priests will have sent runners to the villages to say that you are only men. Why didn't you stick on as Gods till things was more settled? I'm a dead man,' says Billy Fish, and he throws himself down on the snow and begins to pray to his Gods.

"Next morning we was in a cruel bad country —all up and down, no level ground at all, and no food either. The six Bashkai men looked at Billy Fish hungry-wise as if they wanted to ask something, but they said never a word. At noon we came to the top of a flat mountain all covered with snow, and when we climbed up into it, behold, there was an Army in position waiting in the middle!

" 'The runners have been very quick,' says Billy Fish, with a little bit of a laugh. 'They are waiting for us.'

"Three or four men began to fire from the enemy's side, and a chance shot took Daniel in the calf of the leg. That brought him to his senses. He looks across the snow at the Army, and sees the rifles that we had brought into the country.

" 'We're done for,' says he. 'They are Englishmen, these people,—and it's my blasted nonsense that has brought you to this. Get back, Billy Fish, and take your men away; you've done what you could, and now cut for it. Carnehan,' says he, 'shake hands with me and go along with Billy. Maybe they won't kill you. I'll go and meet 'em alone. It's me that did it. Me, the King!'

" 'Go!' says I. 'Go to Hell, Dan! I'm with you here. Billy Fish, you clear out, and we two will meet those folk.'

" 'I'm a Chief,' says Billy Fish, quite quiet. 'I stay with you. My men can go.'

"The Bashkai fellows didn't wait for a second word but ran off, and Dan and Me and Billy Fish walked across to where the drums were drumming and the horns were horning. It was cold—awful cold. I've got that cold in the back of my head now. There's a lump of it there."

The punkah-coolies had gone to sleep. Two kerosene lamps were blazing in the office, and the perspiration poured down my face and splashed on the blotter as I leaned forward. Carnehan was shivering, and I feared that his mind might go. I wiped my face, took a fresh grip of the piteously mangled hands, and said:—"What happened after that?"

The momentary shift of my eyes had broken the clear current.

"What was you pleased to say?" whined Carnehan. "They took them without any sound. Not a little whisper all along the snow, not though the King knocked down the first man that set hand on him—not though old Peachey fired his last cartridge into the brown of 'em. Not a single solitary sound did those swines make. They just closed up tight, and I tell you their furs stunk. There was a man called Billy Fish, a good friend of us all, and they cut his throat, Sir, then and there, like a pig; and the King kicks up the bloody snow and says:—'We've had a dashed fine run for our money. What's coming next?' But Peachey, Peachey Taliaferro, I tell you, Sir, in confidence as betwixt two friends, he lost his head, Sir. No, he didn't neither. The King lost his head, so he did, all along o' one of those cunning rope-bridges. Kindly let me have the paper-cutter, Sir. It tilted this way. They marched him a mile across that snow to a rope-bridge over a ravine with a river at the bottom. You may have seen such. They prodded him behind like an ox. 'Damn your eyes!' says the King. 'D'you suppose I can't die like a gentleman?' He turns to Peachey—Peachey that was crying like a child. 'I've brought you to this, Peachey,' says he. 'Brought you out of your happy life to be killed in

Kafiristan, where you was late Commander-in-Chief of the Emperor's forces. Say you forgive me, Peachey.' 'I do,' says Peachey. 'Fully and freely do I forgive you, Dan.' 'Shake hands, Peachey,' says he. 'I'm going now.' Out he goes, looking neither right nor left, and when he was plumb in the middle of those dizzy dancing ropes, 'Cut, you beggars,' he shouts; and they cut, and old Dan fell, turning round and round and round, twenty thousand miles, for he took half an hour to fall till he struck the water, and I could see his body caught on a rock with the gold crown close beside.

"But do you know what they did to Peachey between two pine trees? They crucified him, Sir, as Peachey's hands will show. They used wooden pegs for his hands and his feet, and he didn't die. He hung there and screamed, and they took him down next day, and said it was a miracle that he wasn't dead. They took him down—poor old Peachey that hadn't done them any harm—that hadn't done them any . . . "

He rocked to and fro and wept bitterly, wiping his eyes with the back of his scarred hands and moaning like a child for some ten minutes.

"They was cruel enough to feed him up in the temple, because they said he was more of a God than old Daniel that was a man. Then they turned him out on the snow, and told him to go home, and Peachey came home in about a year, begging along the roads quite safe; for Daniel

Dravot he walked before and said:—'Come along, Peachey. It's a big thing we're doing.' The mountains they danced at night, and the mountains they tried to fall on Peachey's head, but Dan he held up his hand, and Peachey came along bent double. He never let go of Dan's hand, and he never let go of Dan's head. They gave it to him as a present in the temple, to remind him not to come again, and though the crown was pure gold, and Peachey was starving, never would Peachey sell the same. You knew Dravot, Sir! You knew Right Worshipful Brother Dravot! Look at him now!"

He fumbled in the mass of rags round his bent waist; brought out a black horsehair bag embroidered with silver thread; and shook therefrom on to my table—the dried, withered head of Daniel Dravot! The morning sun that had long been paling the lamps struck the red beard and blind sunken eyes; struck, too, a heavy circlet of gold studded with raw turquoises, that Carnehan placed tenderly on the battered temples.

"You behold now," said Carnehan, "the Emperor in his habit as he lived—the King of Kafiristan with his crown upon his head. Poor old Daniel that was a monarch once!"

I shuddered, for, in spite of defacements manifold, I recognized the head of the man of Marwar Junction. Carnehan rose to go. I attempted to stop him. He was not fit to walk abroad. "Let me take away the whisky, and give me a little money," he gasped. "I was a King once. I'll go to the Deputy Commissioner and ask to set in the Poorhouse till I get my health. No, thank you, I can't wait till you get a carriage for me. I've urgent private affairs—in the south—at Marwar."

He shambled out of the office and departed in the direction of the Deputy Commissioner's house. That day at noon I had occasion to go down the blinding hot Mall, and I saw a crooked man crawling along the white dust of the roadside, his hat in his hand, quavering dolorously after the fashion of street-singers at Home. There was not a soul in sight, and he was out of all possible earshot of the houses. And he sang through his nose, turning his head from right to left:—

> "The Son of Man goes forth to war,
>   A golden crown to gain;
>   His blood-red banner streams afar—
>   Who follows in his train?"

I waited to hear no more, but put the poor wretch into my carriage and drove him off to the nearest missionary for eventual transfer to the Asylum. He repeated the hymn twice while he was with me whom he did not in the least recognize, and I left him singing it to the missionary.

Two days later I inquired after his welfare of the Superintendent of the Asylum.

"He was admitted suffering from sunstroke. He died early yesterday morning," said the Superintendent. "Is it true that he was half an hour bareheaded in the sun at midday?"

"Yes," said I, "but do you happen to know if he had anything upon him by any chance when he died?"

"Not to my knowledge," said the Superintendent.

And there the matter rests.

THE MUTINY OF THE
MAVERICKS

THE MUTINY OF THE MAVERICKS

WHEN three obscure gentlemen in San Francisco argued on insufficient premises, they condemned a fellow-creature to a most unpleasant death in a far country which had nothing whatever to do with the United States. They foregathered at the top of a tenement-house in Tehama Street, an unsavory quarter of the city, and there calling for certain drinks, they conspired because they were conspirators by trade, officially known as the Third Three of the I. A. A.—an institution for the propagation of pure light, not to be confounded with any others, though it is affiliated to many. The Second Three live in Montreal and work among the poor there; the First Three have their home in New York, not far from Castle Garden, and write regularly once a week to a small house near one of the big hotels at Boulogne. What happens after that, a particular section of Scotland Yards knows too well and laughs at. A conspirator detests ridicule. More men have been stabbed with Lucrezia Borgia daggers and dropped into the Thames for laughing at head centers and triangles than for betraying secrets; for this is human nature.

The Third Three conspired over whisky cocktails and a clean sheet of note-paper against the

British Empire and all that lay therein. This work is very like what men without discernment call politics before a general election. You pick out and discuss in the company of congenial friends all the weak points in your opponents' organization, and unconsciously dwell upon and exaggerate all their mishaps, till it seems to you a miracle that the party holds together for an hour.

"Our principle is not so much active demonstration—that we leave to others—as passive embarrassment to weaken and unnerve," said the first man. "Wherever an organization is crippled, wherever a confusion is thrown into any branch of any department, we gain a step for those who take on the work; we are but the forerunners." He was a German enthusiast, and editor of a newspaper, from whose leading articles he quoted frequently.

"That cursed empire makes so many blunders of her own that unless we doubled the year's average I guess it wouldn't strike her anything special had occurred," said the second man. "Are you prepared to say that all our resources are equal to blowing off the muzzle of a hundred-ton gun or spiking a ten-thousand-ton ship on a plain rock in clear daylight? They can beat us at our game. Better join hands with the practical branches; we're in funds now. Try and direct a scare in a crowded street. They value their greasy hides." He was the drag upon the wheel, and an Americanized Irishman of the second generation, despising his own race and hating the other. He had learned caution.

The third man drank his cocktail and spoke no word. He was the strategist, but unfortunately his knowledge of life was limited. He picked a letter from his breast-pocket and threw it across the table. That epistle to the heathen contained some very concise directions from the First Three in New York. It said:

"The boom in black iron has already affected the eastern markets, where our agents have been forcing down the English-held stock among the smaller buyers who watch the turn of shares. Any immediate operations, such as western bears, would increase their willingness to unload. This, however, can not be expected till they see clearly that foreign ironmasters are willing to co-operate. Mulcahy should be dispatched to feel the pulse of the market, and act accordingly. Mavericks are at present the best for our purpose.—P. D. Q."

As a message referring to an iron crisis in Pennsylvania it was interesting, if not lucid. As a new departure in organized attack on an outlying English dependency, it was more than interesting.

The first man read it through, and murmured:

"Already? Surely they are in too great a hurry. All that Dhulip Singh could do in India he has done, down to the distribution of his photographs among the peasantry. Ho! Ho! The

Paris firm arranged that, and he has no substantial money back from the Other Power. Even our agents in India know he hasn't. What is the use of our organization wasting men on work that is already done? Of course, the Irish regiments in India are half mutinous as they stand."

This shows how near a lie may come to the truth. An Irish regiment, for just so long as it stands still, is generally a hard handful to control, being reckless and rough. When, however, it is moved in the direction of musketry-fire, it becomes strangely and unpatriotically content with its lot. It has even been heard to cheer the queen with enthusiasm on these occasions.

But the notion of tampering with the army was, from the point of view of Tehama Street, an altogether sound one. There is no shadow of stability in the policy of an English government, and the most sacred oaths of England would, even if embossed on vellum, find very few buyers among colonies and dependencies that have suffered from vain beliefs. But there remains to England always her army. That can not change, except in the matter of uniform and equipment. The officers may write to the papers demanding the heads of the Horse Guards in default of cleaner redress for grievances; the men may break loose across a country town, and seriously startle the publicans, but neither officers nor men have it in their composition to mutiny after the Continental manner. The English people, when they trouble to think about the army at all, are, and with justice, absolutely assured that it is absolutely trustworthy. Imagine for a moment their emotions on realizing that such and such a regiment was in open revolt from causes directly due to England's management of Ireland. They would probably send the regiments to the polls forthwith, and examine their own conscience as to their duty to Erin, but they would never be easy any more. And it was this vague, unhappy mistrust that the I. A. A. was laboring to produce.

"Sheer waste of breath," said the second man, after a pause in the council. "I don't see the use of tampering with their fool-army, but it has been tried before, and we must try it again. It looks well in the reports. If we send one man from here, you may bet your life that other men are going too. Order up Mulcahy."

They ordered him up—a slim, slight, dark-haired young man, devoured with that blind, rancorous hatred of England that only reaches its full growth across the Atlantic. He had sucked it from his mother's breast in the little cabin at the back of the northern avenues of New York; he had been taught his rights and his wrongs, in German and Irish, on the canal fronts of Chicago; and San Francisco held men who told him strange and awful things of the great blind power over the seas. Once, when business took him across the Atlantic, he had served in an English regiment, and being insubordinate, had suffered extremely. He drew all his ideas of England that were not bred by the cheaper patriotic print, from one iron-fisted colonel and an unbending adjutant. He would go to the mines if need be to teach his gospel. And he went as his instructions advised, p. d. q.—which meant "with speed"—to introduce embarrassment into an Irish regiment, "already half mutinous, quartered among Sikh peasantry, all wearing miniatures of His Highness Dhulip Singh, Maharaja of the Punjab, next their hearts, and all eagerly expecting his arrival." Other information equally valuable was given him by his masters. He was to be cautious, but never to grudge expense in winning the hearts of the men in the regiment. His mother in New York would supply funds, and he was to write to her once a month. Life is pleasant for a man who has a mother in New York to send him £200 a year over and above his regimental pay.

In process of time, thanks to his intimate knowledge of drill and musketry exercise, the excellent Mulcahy, wearing the corporal's stripe, went out in a troop-ship and joined Her Majesty's Royal Loyal Musketeers, commonly known as the "Mavericks," because they were masterless and unbranded cattle—sons of small farmers in County Clare, shoeless vagabonds of Kerry, herders of Ballyvegan, much wanted "moonlighters" from the bare rainy headlands of the south coast,

officered by O'Mores, Bradys' Hills, Kilreas, and
the like. Never, to outward seeming, was there
more promising material to work on. The First
Three had chosen their regiment well. It feared
nothing that moved or talked save the colonel
and the regimental Roman Catholic chaplain, the
fat Father Dennis, who held the keys of heaven
and hell, and glared like an angry bull when he
desired to be convincing. Him also it loved because on occasion of stress he was wont to tuck
up his cassock and charge with the rest into the
merriest of the fray, where he always found,
good man, that the saints sent him a revolver
when there was a fallen private to be protected
or—but this came as an after-thought—his own
gray head to be guarded.

Cautiously as he had been instructed, tenderly
and with much beer, Mulcahy opened his projects
to such as he deemed fittest to listen. And these
were, one and all, of that quaint, crooked, sweet,
profoundly irresponsible, and profoundly lovable
race that fight like fiends, argue like children,
reason like women, obey like men, and jest like
their own goblins of the wrath through rebellion,
loyalty, want, woe, or war. The underground
work of a conspiracy is always dull, and very
much the same the world over. At the end of six
months—the seed always falling on good ground
—Mulcahy spoke almost explicitly, hinting
darkly in the approved fashion at dread powers
behind him, and advising nothing more nor less

than mutiny. Were they not dogs, evilly treated? had they not all their own and the natural revenges to satisfy? Who in these days could do aught to nine hundred men in rebellion? who, again, could stay them if they broke for the sea, licking up on their way other regiments only too anxious to join? And afterward . . . here followed windy promises of gold and preferment, office and honor, ever dear to a certain type of Irishman.

As he finished his speech, in the dusk of a twilight, to his chosen associates, there was a sound of a rapidly unslung belt behind him. The arm of one Dan Grady flew out in the gloom and arrested something. Then said Dan:

"Mulcahy, you're a great man, an' you do credit to whoever sent you. Walk about a bit while we think of it." Mulcahy departed elated. He knew his words would sink deep.

"Why the triple-dashed asterisks did ye not let me curl the tripes out of him?" grunted a voice.

"Because I'm not a fat-headed fool. Boys, 'tis what he's been driving at these six months—our superior copril, with his education, and his copies of the Irish papers, and his everlasting beer. He's been sent for the purpose, and that's where the money comes from. Can ye not see? That man's a gold-mine, which Horse Egan here would have destroyed with a belt-buckle. It would be throwing away the gifts of Providence not to fall in with his little plans. Of course we'll mutiny till all's dry. Shoot the colonel on the parade-ground, massacre the company officers, ransack the arsenal, and then—boys, did he tell you what next? He told me the other night, when he was beginning to talk wild. Then we're to join with the niggers, and look for help from Dhulip Singh and the Russians!"

"And spoil the best campaign that ever was this side of hell! Danny, I'd have lost the beer to ha' given him the belting he requires."

"Oh, let him go this awhile, man! He's got no —no constructiveness; but that's the egg-meat of his plan, and you must understand that I'm in with it, an' so are you. We'll want oceans of beer to convince us—firmaments full. We'll give him talk for his money, and one by one all the boys'll come in, and he'll have a nest of nine hundred mutineers to squat in an' give drink to."

"What makes me killing mad is his wanting us to do what the niggers did thirty years gone. That an' his pig's cheek in saying that other regiments would come along," said a Kerry man.

"That's not so bad as hintin' we should loose off at the colonel."

"Colonel be sugared! I'd as soon as not put a shot through his helmet, to see him jump and clutch his old horse's head. But Mulcahy talks o' shootin' our comp'ny orf'cers accidental."

"He said that, did he?" said Horse Egan.

"Somethin' like that, anyways. Can't ye fancy

ould Barber Brady wid a bullet in his lungs, coughin' like a sick monkey an' sayin': "Bhoys, I do not mind your gettin' dhrunk, but you must hould your liquor like men. The man that shot me is dhrunk. I'll suspend investigations for six hours, while I get this bullet cut out, and then—' "

"An' then," continued Horse Egan, for the peppery major's peculiarities of speech and manner were as well known as his tanned face—"an' then, ye dissolute, half-baked, putty-faced scum o' Connemara, if I find a man so much as lookin' confused, bedad I'll coort-martial the whole company. A man that can't get over his liquor in six hours is not fit to belong to the Mavericks!"

A shout of laughter bore witness to the truth of the sketch.

"It's pretty to think of," said the Kerry man slowly. "Mulcahy would have us do all the devilment, and get clear himself, someways. He wudn't be takin' all this fool's throuble in shpoilin' the reputation of the regiment."

"Reputation of your grandmother's pig!" said Dan.

"Well, an' he had a good reputation, too; so it's all right. Mulcahy must see his way clear out behind him, or he'd not ha' come so far, talkin' powers of darkness."

"Did you hear anything of a regimental court-martial among the Black Boneens, these days? Half a company of 'em took one of the new draft an' hanged him by his arms with a tent-rope from a third-story veranda.   They gave no reason for so doin' but he was half dead.   I'm thinking that the Boneens are short-sighted.   It was a friend of Mulcahy's, or a man in the same trade.   They'd a deal better ha' taken his beer," returned Dan, reflectively.

"Better still ha' handed him up to the colonel," said Horse Egan, "onless——   But sure the news wud be all over the counthry an' give the reg'ment a bad name."

"An' there'd be no reward for that man—but he went about talkin'," said the Kerry man, artlessly.

"You speak by your breed," said Dan, with a laugh.   "There was never a Kerry man yet that wudn't sell his brother for a pipe o' tobacco an' a pat on the back from a policeman."

"Thank God I'm not a bloomin' Orangeman," was the answer.

"No, nor never will be," said Dan.   "They breed men in Ulster.   Would you like to thry the taste of one?"

The Kerry man looked and longed, but forebore.   The odds of battle were too great.

"Then you'll not even give Mulcahy a—a strike for his money," said the voice of Horse Egan, who regarded what he called "trouble" of any kind as the pinnacle of felicity.

Dan answered not at all, but crept on tiptoe, with large strides, to the mess-room, the men fol-

'lowing. The room was empty. In a corner, cased like the King of Dahomey's state umbrella, stood the regimental colors. Dan lifted them tenderly, and unrolled in the light of the candles the record of the Mavericks—tattered, worn, and hacked. The white satin was darkened everywhere with big brown stains, the gold threads on the crowned harp were frayed and discolored, and the red bull, the totem of the Mavericks, was coffee-hued. The stiff, embroidered folds, whose price is human life, rustled down slowly. The Mavericks keep their colors long and guard them very sacredly.

"Vittoria, Salamanca, Toulouse, Waterloo, Moodkee, Ferozshah, and Sobraon—that was fought close next door here, against the very beggars he wants us to join. Inkermann, the Alma, Sebastopol! What are those little businesses compared to the campaigns of General Mulcahy? The mut'ny, think o' that; the mut'ny an' some dirty little matters in Afghanistan, and for that an' these and those"—Dan pointed to the names of glorious battles—"that Yankee man with the partin' in his hair comes and says as easy as 'have a drink' . . . Holy Moses! there's the captain!"

But it was the mess-sergeant who came in just as the men clattered out, and found the colors uncased.

From that day dated the mutiny of the Mavericks, to the joy of Mulcahy and the pride of his

mother in New York—the good lady who sent
the money for the beer. Never, as far as words
went, was such a mutiny. The conspirators, led
by Dan Grady and Horse Egan, poured in daily.
They were sound men, men to be trusted, and they
all wanted blood; but first they must have beer.
They cursed the queen, they mourned over Ireland, they suggested hideous plunder of the Indian country-side, and then, alas! some of the
younger men would go forth and wallow on the
ground in spasms of unholy laughter. The genius
of the Irish for conspiracies is remarkable. None
the less, they would swear no oaths but those of
their own making, which were rare and curious,
and they were always at pains to impress Mulcahy with the risks they ran. Naturally the flood
of beer wrought demoralization. But Mulcahy
confused the causes of things, and when a pot-
valiant Maverick smote a servant on the nose or
called his commanding officer a bald-headed old
lard-bladder, and even worse names, he fancied
that rebellion and not liquor was at the bottom
of the outbreak. Other gentlemen who have con-
cerned themselves in larger conspiracies have
made the same error.

The hot season, in which they protested no man
could rebel, came to an end, and Mulcahy suggested a visible return for his teachings. As to
the actual upshot of the mutiny he cared nothing.
It would be enough if the English, infatuatedly
trusting to the integrity of their army, should be

startled with news of an Irish regiment revolting from political considerations. His persistent demands would have ended, at Dan's instigation, in a regimental belting which in all probability would have killed him and cut off the supply of beer, had not he been sent on special duty some fifty miles away from the cantonment to cool his heels in a mud fort and dismount obsolete artillery. Then the colonel of the Mavericks, reading his newspaper diligently and scenting frontier trouble from afar, posted to the army headquarters and pleaded with the commander-in-chief for certain privileges, to be granted under certain contingencies; which contingencies came about only a week later when the annual little war on the border developed itself and the colonel returned to carry the good news to the Mavericks. He held the promise of the chief for active service, and the men must get ready.

On the evening of the same day, Mulcahy, an unconsidered corporal—yet great in conspiracy —returned to cantonments, and heard sounds of strife and howlings from afar off. The mutiny had broken out, and the barracks of the Mavericks were one whitewashed pandemonium. A private tearing through the barrack square gasped in his ear: "Service! Active service! It's a burnin' shame." Oh, joy, the Mavericks had risen on the eve of battle! They would not —noble and royal sons of Ireland!—serve the queen longer. The news would flash through the

country-side and over to England, and he—Mulcahy—the trusted of the Third Three, had
brought about the crash.   The private stood in
the middle of the square and cursed colonel, regiment, officers, and doctor, particularly the doctor,
by his gods.   An orderly of the native cavalry
regiment clattered through the mob of soldiers.
He was half lifted, half dragged from his horse,
beaten on the back with mighty hand-claps till his
eyes watered, and called all manner of endearing
names.   Yes, the Mavericks had fraternized with
the native troops.   Who, then, was the agent
among the latter that had blindly wrought with
Mulcahy so well?

An officer slunk, almost ran, from the mess to
a barrack.   He was mobbed by the infuriated sol-
diery, who closed round but did not kill him, for
he fought his way to shelter, flying for his life.
Mulcahy could have wept with pure joy and
thankfulness.   The very prisoners in the guard-
room were shaking the bars of their cells
and howling like wild beasts, and from every
barrack poured the booming as of a big war-
drum.

Mulcahy hastened to his own barrack.   He
could hardly hear himself speak.   Eighty men
were pounding with fist and heel the tables and
trestles—eighty men flushed with mutiny, stripped
to their shirt-sleeves, their knapsacks half-packed
for the march to the sea, made the two-inch
boards thunder again as they chanted to a tune

that Mulcahy knew well, the Sacred War Song of the Mavericks:

> "Listen in the north, my boys, there's trouble on
>   the wind;
> Tramp o' Cossacks hoofs in front, gray great-coats
>   behind,
> Trouble on the frontier of a most amazin' kind,
>   Trouble on the water o' the Oxus!"

Then as a table broke under the furious accompaniment:

> Hurrah! hurrah! it's northwest we go;
> Hurrah! hurrah! the chance we wanted so;
> Let 'em hear the chorus from Umballa to Moscow,
>   As we go marching to the Kremlin."

"Mother of all the saints in bliss and all the devils in cinders, where's my fine new sock widout the heel?" howled Horse Egan, ransacking everybody's knapsack but his own. He was engaged in making up deficiencies of kit preparatory to a campaign, and in that employ he steals best who steals last. "Ah, Mulcahy, you're in good time," he shouted. "We've got the route, and we're off Thursday for a picnic wid the Lancers next door."

An ambulance orderly appeared with a huge basket full of lint rolls, provided by the forethought of the queen, for such as might need them later on. Horse Egan unrolled his bandage and flicked it under Mulcahy's nose, chanting:

" 'Sheep's skin an' bees'-wax, thunder, pitch and
  plaster;
The more you try to pull it off, the more it sticks
  the faster,
As I was goin' to New Orleans——'

You know the rest of it, my Irish-American-Jew
boy. By gad, ye have to fight for the queen in the
inside av a fortnight, my darlin'."

A roar of laughter interrupted. Mulcahy
looked vacantly down the room. Bid a boy defy
his father when the pantomime-cab is at the door,
or a girl develop a will of her own when her
mother is putting the last touches to the first ball-
dress, but do not ask an Irish regiment to embark
upon mutiny on the eve of a campaign; when it
has fraternized with the native regiment that accompanies it, and driven its officers into retire-
ment with ten thousand clamorous questions, and
the prisoners dance for joy, and the sick men
stand in the open, calling down all known diseases on the head of the doctor who has certified
that they are "medically unfit for active service."
And even the Mavericks might have been mistaken for mutineers by one so unversed in their
natures as Mulcahy. At dawn a girls' school
might have learned deportment from them. They
knew that their colonel's hand had closed, and
that he who broke that iron discipline would not
go to the front. Nothing in the world will per-
suade one of our soldiers when he is ordered to
the north on the smallest of affairs, that he is not

immediately going gloriously to slay Cossacks and cook his kettles in the palace of the czar. A few of the younger men mourned for Mulcahy's beer, because the campaign was to be conducted on strict temperance principles, but, as Dan and Horse Egan said sternly: "We've got the beer-man with us; he shall drink now on his own hook."

Mulcahy had not taken into account the possibility of being sent on active service. He had made up his mind that he would not go under any circumstances; but fortune was against him.

"Sick—you?" said the doctor, who had served an unholy apprenticeship to his trade in Tralee poor-houses. "You're only homesick, and what you call varicose veins come from overeating. A little gentle exercise will cure that." And later: "Mulcahy, my man, everybody is allowed to apply for a sick certificate once. If he tries it twice, we call him by an ugly name. Go back to your duty, and let's hear no more of your diseases."

I am ashamed to say that Horse Egan enjoyed the study of Mulcahy's soul in those days, and Dan took an equal interest. Together they would communicate to their corporal all the dark lore of death that is the portion of those who have seen men die. Egan had the larger experience, but Dan the finer imagination. Mulcahy shivered when the former spoke of the knife as an intimate acquaintance, or the latter dwelt with loving particularity on the fate of those who, wounded

and helpless, had been overlooked by the ambu-
lances, and had fallen into the hands of the Afghan women-folk.

Mulcahy knew that the mutiny, for the present
at least, was dead. Knew, too, that a change had
come over Dan's usually respectful attitude toward him, and Horse Egan's laughter and frequent allusions to abortive conspiracies empha-
sized all that the conspirator had guessed. The
horrible fascination of the death-stories, however, made him seek their society. He learned
much more than he had bargained for; and in
this manner. It was on the last night before the
regiment entrained to the front. The barracks
were stripped of everything movable, and the men
were too excited to sleep. The bare walls gave
out a heavy hospital smell of chloride of lime—a
stench that depresses the soul.

"And what," said Mulcahy in an awe-stricken
whisper, after some conversation on the eternal
subject, "are you going to do to me, Dan?" This
might have been the language of an able conspirator conciliating a weak spirit.

"You'll see," said Dan, grimly, turning over in
his cot, "or I rather shud say you'll not see."

This was hardly the language of a weak spirit.
Mulcahy shook under the bed-clothes.

"Be easy with him," put in Egan from the next
cot. "He has got his chanst o' goin' clean.
Listen, Mulcahy: all we want is for the good sake
of the regiment that you take your death stand-

ing up, as a man shud. There be heaps an' heaps of enemy—plenshus heaps. Go there an' do all you can and die decent. You'll die with a good name there. 'Tis not a hard thing considerin'."

Again Mulcahy shivered.

"And how could a man wish to die better than fightin'?" added Dan, consolingly.

"And if I won't?" said the corporal in a dry whisper.

"There'll be a dale of smoke," returned Dan, sitting up and ticking off the situation on his fingers, "sure to be, an' the noise of the firin' 'll be tremenjus, an' we'll be running about up and down, the regiment will. But we, Horse and I— we'll stay by you, Mulcahy, and never let you go. Maybe there'll be an accident."

"It's playing it low on me. Let me go. For pity's sake, let me go! I never did you harm, and —and I stood you as much beer as I could. Oh, don't be so hard on me, Dan! You are—you were in it, too. You won't kill me up there, will you?"

"I'm not thinkin' of the treason; though you shud be glad any honest boys drank with you. It's for the regiment. We can't have the shame o' you bringin' shame on us. You went to the doctor quiet as a sick cat to get and stay behind an' live with the women at the depot—you that wanted us to run to the sea in wolf-packs like the rebels none of your black blood dared to be! But we knew about your goin' to the doctor, for he

told it in mess, and it's all over the regiment.
Bein' as we are your best friends, we didn't allow
any one to molest you yet. We will see to you
ourselves. Fight which you will—us or the enemy
—you'll never lie in that cot again, and there's
more glory and maybe less kicks from fighting
the enemy. That's fair speakin'."

"And he told us by word of mouth to go and
join with the niggers—you've forgotten that,
Dan," said Horse Egan, to justify sentence.

"What's the use of plaguin' the man? One
shot pays for all. Sleep ye sound, Mulcahy. But
you onderstand, do ye not?"

Mulcahy for some weeks understood very little
of anything at all save that ever at his elbow, in
camp, or at parade, stood two big men with soft
voices adjuring him to commit *hari kari* lest a
worse thing should happen—to die for the honor
of the regiment in decency among the nearest
knives. But Mulcahy dreaded death. He remembered certain things that priests had said in
his infancy, and his mother—not the one at New
York—starting from her sleep with shrieks to
pray for a husband's soul in torment. It is well
to be of a cultured intelligence, but in time of
trouble the weak human mind returns to the creed
it sucked in at the breast, and if that creed be
not a pretty one, trouble follows. Also, the death
he would have to face would be physically painful. Most conspirators have large imaginations.
Mulcahy could see himself, as he lay on the earth

in the night, dying by various causes. They were
all horrible; the mother in New York was very
far away, and the regiment, the engine that,
once you fall in its grip, moves you forward
whether you will or won't, was daily coming
closer to the enemy!

*　　*　　*　　*　　*　　*

They were brought to the field of Mazun-Katai,
and with the Black Boneens to aid, they fought a
fight that has never been set down in the newspapers. In response, many believe, to the fervent
prayers of Father Dennis, the enemy not only
elected to fight in the open, but made a beautiful
fight, as many weeping Irish mothers knew later.
They gathered behind walls or flickered across
the open in shouting masses, and were pot-valiant
in artillery. It was expedient to hold a large reserve and wait for the psychological moment that
was being prepared by the shrieking shrapnel.
Therefore the Mavericks lay down in open order
on the brow of a hill to watch the play till their
call should come. Father Dennis, whose place
was in the rear, to smooth the trouble of the
wounded, had naturally managed to make his way
to the foremost of his boys, and lay, like a black
porpoise, at length on the grass. To him crawled
Mulcahy, ashen-gray, demanding absolution.

"Wait till you're shot," said Father Dennis,
sweetly. "There's a time for everything."

Dan Grady chuckled as he blew for the fiftieth time into the breech of his speckless rifle. Mulcahy groaned and buried his head in his arms till a stray shot spoke like a snipe immediately above his head, and a general heave and tremor rippled the line. Other shots followed, and a few took effect, as a shriek or a grunt attested. The officers, who had been lying down with the men, rose and began to walk steadily up and down the front of their companies.

This maneuver, executed not for publication, but as a guarantee of good faith, to soothe men, demands nerve. You must not hurry, you must not look nervous, though you know that you are a mark for every rifle within extreme range; and, above all, if you are smitten you must make as little noise as possible and roll inward through the files. It is at this hour, when the breeze brings the first salt whiff of the powder to noses rather cold at the tips, and the eye can quietly take in the appearance of each red casualty, that the strain on the nerves is strongest. Scotch regiments can endure for half a day, and abate no whit of their zeal at the end; English regiments sometimes sulk under punishment, while the Irish, like the French, are apt to run forward by ones and twos, which is just as bad as running back. The truly wise commandant of highly strung troops allows them in seasons of waiting to hear the sound of their own voices uplifted in song. There is a legend of an English regiment that lay by its arms under fire chanting "Sam Hall," to the horror of its newly appointed and pious colonel. The Black Boneens, who were suffering more than the Mavericks, on a hill half a mile away, began presently to explain to all who cared to listen:

> "We'll sound the jubilee, from the center to the
>   sea,
> And Ireland shall be free, says the Shan-van-
>   Voght.'

"Sing, boys," said Father Dennis, softly. "It looks as if we cared for their Afghan peas."

Dan Grady raised himself to his knees and opened his mouth in a song imparted to him, as to most of his comrades, in the strictest confidence by Mulcahy—that Mulcahy then lying limp and fainting on the grass, the chill fear of death upon him.

Company after company caught up the words which, the I. A. A. say, are to herald the general rising of Erin, and to breathe which, except to those duly appointed to hear, is death. Wherefore they are printed in this place:

> "The Saxon in heaven's just balance is weighed,
>   His doom, like Belshazzar's, in death has been
>   cast,
> And the hand of the 'venger shall never be stayed
>   Till his race, faith, and speech are a dream of
>   the past."

They are heart-filling lines, and they ran with
a swirl; the I. A. A. are better served by
pens than their petards. Dan clapped Mulcahy
merrily on the back, asking him to sing up. The
officers lay down again. There was no need to
walk any more. Their men were soothing themselves, thunderously, thus:

"St. Mary in heaven has written the vow
    That the land shall not rest till the heretic blood,
From the babe at the breast to the hand at the plow,
    Has rolled to the ocean like Shannon in flood!"

"I'll speak to you after all's over," said Father
Dennis, authoritatively, in Dan's ear. "What's
the use of confessing to me when you do this foolishness? Dan, you've been playing with fire! I'll
lay you more penance in a week than—"

"Come along to purgatory with us, father,
dear. The Boneens are on the move; they'll let
us go now!"

The regiment rose to the blast of the bugle
as one man; but one man there was who rose
more swiftly than all the others, for half an
inch of bayonet was in the fleshy part of his
leg.

"You've got to do it," said Dan, grimly. "Do
it decent, anyhow;" and the roar of the rush
drowned his words as the rear companies thrust
forward the first, still singing as they swung
down the slope:

"From the child at the breast to the hand at the plow
Has rolled to the ocean like Shannon in flood!"

They should have sung it in the face of England, not of the Afghans, whom it impressed as much as did the wild Irish yell.

"They came down singing," said the unofficial report of the enemy, borne from village to village next day. "They continued to sing, and it was written that our men could not abide when they came. It is believed that there was magic in the aforesaid song."

Dan and Horse Egan kept themselves in the neighborhood of Mulcahy. Twice the man would have bolted back in the confusion. Twice he was heaved like a half-drowned kitten into the unpaintable inferno of a hotly contested charge.

At the end, the panic excess of his fear drove him into madness beyond all human courage. His eyes staring at nothing, his mouth open and frothing, and breathing as one in a cold bath, he went forward demented, while Dan toiled after him. The charge was checked at a high mud wall. It was Mulcahy that scrambled up tooth and nail and heaved down among the bayonets the amazed Afghan who barred his way. It was Mulcahy, keeping to the straight line of the rabid dog, led a collection of ardent souls at a newly unmasked battery, and flung himself on the muzzle of a gun as his companions danced among the gunners. It was Mulcahy who ran wildly on from that battery into the open plain where the enemy were retiring in sullen groups. His hands were empty, he had lost helmet and belt, and he was bleeding from a wound in the neck. Dan and Horse Egan, panting and distressed, had thrown themselves down on the ground by the captured guns, when they noticed Mulcahy's flight.

"Mad," said Horse Egan, critically. "Mad with fear! He's going straight to his death, an' shoutin's no use."

"Let him go. Watch now! If we fire we'll hit him maybe."

The last of a hurrying crowd of Afghans turned at the noise of shod feet behind him, and shifted his knife ready to hand. This, he saw, was no time to take prisoners. Mulcahy ran on, sobbing, and the straight-held blade went home through the defenseless breast, and the body pitched forward almost before a shot from Dan's rifle brought down the slayer and still further hurried the Afghan retreat. The two Irishmen went out to bring in their dead.

"He was given the point, and that was an easy death," said Horse Egan, viewing the corpse. "But would you ha' shot him, Danny, if he had lived?"

"He didn't live, so there's no sayin'. But I doubt I wud have, bekase of the fun he gave us— let alone the beer. Hike up his legs, Horse, and we'll bring him in. Perhaps 'tis better this way."

They bore the poor limp body to the mass of

the regiment, lolling open-mouthed on their rifles; and there was a general snigger when one of the younger subalterns said: "That was a good man!"

"Phew!" said Horse Egan, when a burial party had taken over the burden. "I'm powerful dhry, and this reminds me, there'll be no more beer at all."

"Fwhy not?" said Dan, with a twinkle in his eye as he stretched himself for a rest. "Are we not conspirin' all we can, an' while we conspire are we not entitled to free dhrinks? Sure his ould mother in New York would not let her son's comrades perish of drouth—if she can be reached at the end of a letter."

"You're a janius," said Horse Egan. "O' coorse she will not. I wish this crool war was over, an' we'd get back to canteen. Faith, the commander-in-chief ought to be hanged on his own little sword-belt for makin' us work on wather."

The Mavericks were generally of Horse Egan's opinion. So they made haste to get their work done as soon as possible, and their industry was rewarded by unexpected peace. "We can fight the sons of Adam," said the tribesmen, "but we can not fight the sons of Eblis, and this regiment never stays still in one place. Let us therefore come in." They came in, and "this regiment" withdrew to conspire under the leadership of Dan Grady.

Excellent as a subordinate, Dan failed altogether as a chief-in-command—possibly because he was too much swayed by the advice of the only man in the regiment who could perpetrate more than one kind of handwriting. The same mail that bore to Mulcahy's mother in New York a letter from the colonel, telling her how valiantly her son had fought for the queen, and how assuredly he would have been recommended for the Victoria Cross had he survived, carried a communication signed, I grieve to say, by that same colonel and all the officers of the regiment, explaining their willingness to do "anything which is contrary to the regulations and all kinds of revolutions" if only a little money could be forwarded to cover incidental expenses. Daniel Grady, Esquire, would receive funds, vice Mulcahy, who "was unwell at this present time of writing."

Both letters were forwarded from New York to Tehema Street, San Francisco, with marginal comments as brief as they were bitter. The Third Three read and looked at each other. Then the Second Conspirator—he who believed in "joining hands with the practical branches"—began to laugh, and on recovering his gravity, said: "Gentlemen, I consider this will be a lesson to us. We're left again. Those cursed Irish have let us down. I knew they would, but"—here he laughed afresh—"I'd give considerable to know what was at the back of it all."

His curiosity would have been satisfied had he seen Dan Grady, discredited regimental conspirator, trying to explain to his thirsty comrades in India the non-arrival of funds from New York.

THE END